"Something wrong?" he asked

"No." Beth's answer was short. Brand didn't want her serving with him; he thought she should have stayed in her safe classroom, teaching languages to kids, out of his way. Her fingers curled instinctively around his as they stood looking out across the water, quiet with the receding tide and the breakers too far out to be heard.

Brand let go of her hand and draped his arm casually around her, his big hand resting at her waist. Beth leaned against him, feeling his hard frame against her softer one. He was well over six feet, making her seem small, especially since she was barefoot, her feet burrowed in the soft sand.

The hand at her waist tightened and he turned her toward him, his other hand going beneath her chin to lift her face.

"No." Beth shook her head.

"This may be my last chance before graduation," he said.

"You don't have to kiss me at all."

"I want to," he countered, holding her so that she could not pull away....

ABOUT THE AUTHOR

Zelma Orr had a most interesting career before turning to writing full-time. Like her heroine in this story, Zelma was a U.S. Customs Officer for the Treasury Department in her home state of Texas. Zelma loves to travel and keeps a diary of the places she has visited to use for story ideas in future books.

Books by Zelma Orr

HARLEQUIN INTRIGUE
12–NIGHT SHADOWS

HARLEQUIN AMERICAN ROMANCE
7–MIRACLES TAKE LONGER
18–IN THE EYES OF LOVE
55–LOVE IS A FAIRY TALE
82–MEASURE OF LOVE

These books may be available at your local bookseller.

Don't miss any of our special offers. Write to us at the following address for information on our newest releases.

Harlequin Reader Service
P.O. Box 52040, Phoenix, AZ 85072-2040
Canadian address: P.O. Box 2800, Postal Station A,
5170 Yonge St., Willowdale, Ont. M2N 6J3

NIGHT SHADOWS

ZELMA ORR

Harlequin Books

TORONTO • NEW YORK • LONDON
AMSTERDAM • PARIS • SYDNEY • HAMBURG
STOCKHOLM • ATHENS • TOKYO • MILAN

Harlequin Intrigue edition published February 1985

ISBN 0-373-22012-X

Chapter One

It was a familiar Saturday night scene. The lights along the street were bright enough to show the not too well kept buildings, the littered sidewalks, the smell of decaying food and bodies hanging heavy in the thick air. The people walking the sidewalks were the hangers-on to the shirttails of life as it passed around or over them.

A drunk mumbled in the doorway of the bar from which he had just been ejected. A young woman, dressed in a low-necked fringed blouse and purple skirt split to her thigh, leaned carelessly against a streetlamp. Her brassy blond hair was piled high on her head, her crimson mouth showing fluorescent in the flickering neon lights. A huge plastic handbag hung over her left arm.

Footsteps sounded in muffled rhythm along the street and the blonde lifted her head, her eyes glowing with interest. She watched a man stride past the drunk still leaning in the doorway, hesitate, then stop in front of her.

His shifty eyes took in her deliberately eye-catching

costume and his tongue licked at the corner of his mouth. "How's tricks, honey?"

"Been better," the blond girl answered with her come-on smile.

The man fingered the pocket of his sweat-stained shirt with dirty fingers, coming forth with a cigarette, lighting it with a wooden match he flicked with a broken thumbnail. He took a long drag from the cigarette and handed it to her.

Smiling, she accepted the smoke, placing it between the thickly painted lips, then rummaged in her handbag, from which she drew a plastic bag which she slipped into his hand.

He reached for the bag, giving it a quick glance, and unbuttoned his shirt to put it underneath just as the drunk from the doorway straightened and moved quickly to his side. In the drunk's hand was a revolver.

"I'll take that," he said firmly and with his free hand flashed identification. "Federal officer."

The man he had confronted half turned as if to run but Beth Page stepped from the shadows to stand beside the "drunk."

She, too, had a gun now pointed at the blond girl. "How much more of the stuff do you have, sis?" she asked.

"That's all," the girl replied nervously.

"You're lying," Beth told her. She reached for the handbag with her free hand but the blonde swung it at her face. At the same time, the man lunged at the "drunk." Beth ducked the purse and pushed the woman against the wall.

She turned to see her partner and the dope peddler

grappling on the sidewalk. The peddler got away from him, recovered the gun and pointed it at the identified officer.

"Shoot, Beth!"

The gun Beth held was now pointed at the sidewalk; there was no strength in her hand to lift it or pull the trigger.

"Your gun! Shoot, damn it, shoot!"

She couldn't even point the gun at the man much less shoot.

THE SOUND OF BACKGROUND COMMOTION and conversation brought Beth back to the present and she drew in a shaky breath, looking around. The lights came on, revealing what might have been a movie set.

It was really a staged confrontation between drug peddlers and Customs Patrol Officers going through advanced training at the Federal Law Enforcement Training Center in Glynco, Georgia. The cadets were exposed to situations designed to approximate what would happen to them in what they affectionately called the "real world."

The two men approached Beth and the one playing her partner in the exercise touched her arm as they stopped beside her. Beth tried to apologize, but she was afraid to open her mouth, busy trying not to cry.

Don Genteel, their instructor, strode across the makeshift stage, his agitation evident in the jerky steps and the fingers plowing through his thinning hair. Students like Beth Page helped cause the loss of that hair, he would be quick to tell anyone who would listen.

"For God's sake, Page, why do you think you were

issued a gun if you weren't intended to use it? A lot of good you'd do Page with him already dead. Page—" He stopped, making an impatient gesture. "Damn it, couldn't you at least have a different name so you could tell who I'm talking to?"

Just the appearance of the instructor served to calm her and Beth looked straight at him as she said, "My father isn't here so permit me to apologize for him."

"What's your father got to do with it?"

"I'm sure he didn't realize the name was taken at the time it was entered on his birth certificate."

A ripple of laughter went through the group gathered around them and Genteel glared.

"All right. Tomorrow in class we'll critique this fiasco." His look took in the group, finally resting on Beth. "At least, it was good for one thing. You've seen a classic example of what not to do when your partner's in trouble."

Beth turned without speaking to anyone and headed for the track around the athletic field where she walked, head down, for ten minutes before turning toward the barrackslike buildings that were the dormitories for the Customs Patrol Officers in training.

Carol Smith, aptly nicknamed Smitty, her roommate, was there ahead of her, already dressing to go out with Ted, one of the officers assigned with them.

Beth flung her weary body across the bed and Smitty followed her actions with her eyes.

"How's tricks?" she asked quietly.

Beth's voice was flat. "Been better."

"Rough show?" Smitty asked, sympathy evident in her voice.

"I'd rather play Wednesday matinees in Philadelphia."

"What happened? The trick get your gun? You forget to read them their rights in both English and Spanish? Your bra snap?"

"I froze."

"Froze?" Smitty echoed, turning to look at her.

"The doper got Brand's gun and pointed it at him. I couldn't move. In real life Brand and I both would be dead. The headlines in my hometown paper would read: 'Beth Page Graduates CPO Academy Sitting Duck Cum Laude.'"

Smitty laughed. "There's your problem, of course. They put you in with the Great God Brand. The Academy's fair-haired boy. I bet you were set up. They probably told him to let the guy get the gun to make you look bad."

Turning back to the mirror, she began to brush her hair, then stopped to watch Beth as she spoke. "You know how they feel about women here. Not just Genteel but all the others, including Brand Page. Just because he has the same last name as you doesn't mean he's on your side."

"He asked me out."

"He what?" she sputtered angrily. "I hope you told him how far out he really was."

Beth sat up. "What I told him was that I'd be pleased and honored to join him for drinks and dinner on Friday night. Of course, that was before I got him killed. I suspect he'll find his hair needs washing Friday. Not that I really blame him."

"You're an idiot, Beth. It could have happened to

anyone; too bad it had to be with Brand as your super partner.''

"Brand's not so bad; a little gung ho maybe.''

"He's so glum. He may only be a Customs Officer, but he's as solemn as a judge.''

Startled, Beth whispered, "As Jud?''

Smitty gave her a worried look. "I didn't mention Jud.''

"I thought you said..." Beth's voice faded.

"I'm sorry; I didn't mean to stir up bad memories.''

"It's okay. After a year, I should be back to normal.''

In her straightforward way, Smitty issued her opinion. "I don't see how replacing him on the Patrol is going to help you get over him.''

"I didn't say I'd ever get over him, Smitty, but didn't you ever take a logic course in college? The Patrol was Jud's life; he was my life. Therefore, the Patrol is also my life. If A equals B and B equals C, then A also equals C. Simple logic.''

"Simpleminded, if you ask me," Smitty told her.

Beth rolled over and lay with her face buried in the pillow until Smitty finished dressing and Ted came by for her. Unwelcome silence left nothing for her to do but think of how she came to be in her present predicament.

Judson Chambers had been the center of her life, the beginning and the end since Beth could remember. A year ago he was killed in a shootout with drug smugglers in Miami, giving his life to protect his teammates. Coming out of the endless blackness following his death, she discussed going into the Customs Patrol with her parents. Although they didn't approve entirely of her choice, they gave their support when she left her position as language instructor in the Macon school system and joined as one of the first women in the unique Patrol.

It had not been easy; nor had she expected it to be. No word was spoken in her hearing against her, but the coolness, the wariness, was there. She understood. Jud had never discussed the numerous dangers he faced; had never allowed her to be touched by the dirty jobs they were called on to do; had always protected her, loved her—and now had left her alone.

During her three-month orientation period in Jacksonville waiting for her background field investigation to be completed, she had studied, had read everything there was in the technical library about the duties of the Customs Patrol. And the more she read, the more she understood the reluctance of the men to accept a woman into their ranks. She might be willing; she might be intelligent; but she did not—could not—have the strength that might some day be required of her to save her life or that of someone else.

The heaviness in her chest threatened to smother her and she rolled over to stare at the ceiling. Beth Page was not given to attacks of nerves, but she strongly suspected that was what was happening in her slender body at that moment.

She jumped as a sharp knock came at the door but she didn't get up nor ask who it was. After a second rap, she heard Brandon Page's deep voice. "Beth?"

Still she didn't answer and a moment later she heard the door across the hall open and close—to the room Brand shared with Johnny West.

Brandon Page was one of the officers who did not approve of women in the Patrol. Dark eyes in a thin face showed that disapproval and she wondered at his asking her to go out. Older than most of the class, probably in his early or mid-thirties, he was quietly attentive to everything that went on and at the head of the class in most courses. Their confrontations, so far, had been relatively friendly, but after today when she caused him to be killed . . . perhaps that would change.

Chapter Two

The track was empty and Beth started out at a slow running pace in the near darkness. Heavy storm clouds hid the sun trying to come over the trees behind the dormitory, but she paid no attention. She moved at a furious pace, running from her own demons, wiping sweat from her face at regular intervals.

She became aware of a second set of footsteps and turned toward the sound to see Brand coming behind her. He came even with her and they ran in silence. After a complete lap, she slowed to a walk, breathing hard.

"You should have been here earlier; it wasn't so crowded."

"Crowds like this don't bother me," he told her. "I got used to it playing football."

"You played football?"

"Sure. In high school."

Curiosity got the better of her. "Where was that?" They had been in classes more or less together for almost twelve weeks and she knew nothing about the man who, strangely enough, had the same last name as hers as well as the same first initial.

"Patagonia," he said.

"You played football in Argentina?"

He laughed. "Patagonia, Arizona."

She waited and when he didn't elaborate on that location, she said, "Okay, okay. I'll bite."

"It's on the Mexican border, south of Tucson. Half the people and all the cattle in the area came to see me play."

"Were you any good?"

"The cows thought so. You should've heard them bellow when I scored a touchdown."

"You're nuts," she said, laughing in spite of herself. They were quiet for a moment and she stared up at the threatening clouds, commenting, "Nice."

"Nice? Those clouds look angry at somebody to me."

"Well, you could be right. It's hurricane season."

Brand eyed the darkness above them. "I've never been in a hurricane. Don't know if I'd care to be either."

"I can tell you they're no fun," she assured him.

"Speaking of fun, classes will be starting soon. We'd better get changed." He started away.

"What are you doing out here running anyway? I've been out here every morning since I got to this madhouse and you've never been here at this time. Why today?"

"I wanted to talk to you," he said.

"Well, let's talk."

"We did. Or didn't you notice?"

"You know what I mean. You had something on your mind; what is it?"

He smiled down at her and touched her wet hair where it clung to her cheeks. "It'll keep till Friday night."

"You mean you still want to go out with me?" she asked unable to mask her genuine surprise.

"Of course. Why wouldn't I?"

"I mean . . . Well, after last night . . ."

He nodded. "We can talk about that. Come on; we'd better move or Genteel will have something else to yell about."

CLASSES WITH GENTEEL were never dull no matter what else they might be. He shot questions at them, threw them into situations she was sure no one on earth would ever face, fought with them right down the line to make them understand it was a life-and-death situation.

"Your life depends on it, Smith," he yelled at Smitty as she hesitated before answering the question he directed at her. "Not only your life, but that of Page or Thorpe or Duran." He stood over her and his voice grew deceptively gentle. "They don't give you time to think it over, Smith. They don't give a damn if you leave a loving husband behind or four kids."

He walked back to the front of the class and said, "It's entirely up to you whether you live or die out there."

The hair on Beth's neck rose beneath the collar of her dark blue shirt. She was staring at the goose bumps on her arms when he said quietly, "Buses are waiting to take you to the firing range. All of you had damn sure better qualify with those weapons if you want to pass this course."

She and Smitty sat side by side for the ride to the firing range in the swamp back of the base, neither of them speaking. The long twelve-week course was coming down to the wire and they were tired. And uneasy.

Still in silence, they put on the protective head gear, checked their weapons, and assumed positions for firing. Beth was good; she didn't have to worry about qualifying. She fired without thinking. It was the best way she had found to handle the .357 Magnum weapon they used. It was heavy; it was ugly; if she didn't think about what happened at the other end of that bullet, she could manage without any trouble.

Removing the protective gear from her ears as she saw her scores go up, she moved away from the firing line to see Brand waiting for her.

"You're pretty good with that," he said.

"You mean when there's only a cardboard target and not another person at the end of the barrel?"

Brand studied her face turned up toward his. Her silvery ash-blond hair was damp with perspiration, clinging to her neck and cheeks, almost matching the silvery gray of her eyes. Sooty lashes cast shadows into the light color, giving them an odd two-toned look. The short nose turned up ever so slightly, a few freckles straying across the narrow bridge. Her lips were parted a little as she waited for him to speak.

"Was last night the first time you've ever seen another person at the end of the barrel?"

Beth nodded. "Until I came here, I'd never even held a gun and I don't like it one bit."

"Your best shots are usually those who have never shot before. They don't have as much to unlearn."

She pondered that a moment but before she could come up with a bright answer, the firing was over and they loaded back on the buses for the return trip.

"Pick you up at seven thirty?" he asked as he stood behind her.

She nodded, feeling the touch of his hand on her arm as she stepped up on the bus.

"You're really going out with him?" Smitty asked, watching Beth brush out her thick hair.

"I've lost five pounds since I got here and I'm sure it's the cafeteria, not the exercise." In the jeans and peasant-necked white blouse, gathered enough to add fullness to her small breasts, she looked as though she had lost a lot of weight. Her body was tight and strong, her build naturally slender; she was five feet six inches tall, weighing about a hundred and fifteen pounds.

She grinned at Smitty as she put her brush down. "I want a steak; maybe shrimp."

"Rough choice," Smitty said.

"You and Ted going out?"

"Yeah. I can't decide whether to have the Big Mac or the Quarter Pounder."

As she laughed at Smitty, Beth suddenly remembered the mail. "Didn't we get anything in the mail today?"

"Nope. I checked three times."

"Don't most classes get their assignments in the mail now?"

"With all the cutbacks plus the transfers to Florida, probably nobody knows where anybody is at any time. Besides, you can bet that you and I will be the last ones to get assignments. Nobody with any pull is going to take a female CPO."

Beth chewed her lip. "You're probably right. And maybe they're right not to want us. Maybe we don't belong in the Patrol."

"There's a place for us. We can do the job," Smitty assured her.

"I couldn't even pretend to shoot that gun in the exercise the other night, Smitty. Suppose I never was able to do it?"

"I know you better than that. You always know what to do and you do it; that's why you're here in the first place."

Her doubtful reply was interrupted by a knock at the door. "I wonder if that's steak or Big Mac?" Smitty said.

Stifling her giggle, Beth called, "Who is it?"

"Brand."

"What do you know? It's neither one—it's a breakfast cereal," Smitty said.

Laughing now, Beth picked up her purse, going to the door. "See you." She smiled at Brand as she dropped her key into her handbag, looking over his tall slim figure in jeans almost matching hers.

He held her elbow as they walked silently down the hall.

The silence stretched between them as he opened the car door for her and entered the driver's side, pulling from the parking lot before he looked at her. Deep in thought, she didn't notice the several looks he directed at her.

He coughed, but she didn't appear to notice. "Beth?"

The sound of acknowledgment she made didn't move her from her own little world that still surrounded her.

"Hello? Beth? Are you with me?"

She stirred reluctantly and turned to meet his quizzical dark gray gaze, darker than hers. "Brand, what do you think about women Patrol officers?"

"Ah, you are alive," he concluded.

"Yes, and I want to stay that way." She drew in her breath. "I want to stay alive, Brand, and that's why I asked. Do you really believe I can hold my own in this outfit?"

"I'm not against equal rights, but—"

"Don't patronize me. Just give me a straight answer."

"Then no. No, I don't think any woman should be in the Customs Patrol."

"You wouldn't want a woman serving next to you?"

He was quiet for a heartbeat. "No."

She had asked for his opinion and gotten it, and somehow it was an opinion she respected. She didn't wholeheartedly agree with it, but she respected it.

Maybe I do agree with him, she thought, silently gazing out the window of the car, seeing only Brand's reflection opposite her. *I should be filled with self-righteous anger but . . .*

Realizing the car had stopped, she straightened in the seat and slid out without looking at him when he opened her door, walking into the restaurant beside him, not touching, not speaking.

As they were seated and menus placed in front of them, she looked up to find Brand's dark gaze on her. He smiled, his eyes going to her lips an instant and back, an odd expression in them that she wouldn't dare try to interpret.

"I told Smitty I wouldn't be able to decide between steak and seafood," she said, keeping her voice casual.

"They have a steak and shrimp platter. So have both."

"Sold. Medium on the steak."

The waitress returned and Brand gave their order, adding, "And two whiskey sours, please." Looking at her, he said, "So you have doubts about being in this business?"

She studied the tanned face in front of her. His dark hair was generously mixed with gray, brows thick and dark above the dark gray eyes fringed by stubby lashes. His face was too thin for handsomeness. His mouth...

Meeting his gaze, she ignored his question, and asked, "How did you know I'd want a whiskey sour?"

"You seemed the type."

"Because I'm in a sour mood?"

"Does thinking about the Patrol put you in a sour mood?"

"I had a moment's weakness, Brand. Don't you ever have any doubts about yourself?"

"If you have doubts now, what's it going to be like when you get out into the real thing?"

She stiffened. "You won't let me forget how I froze in that exercise, will you?"

"Trust is everything. If you can't trust your partner, you may as well stay home."

"Maybe I should have stayed home tonight."

The waitress placed their drinks in front of them and Brand lifted his glass to her. "Here's to home. May it always be there when you need it and may you always be there when you should be."

Her eyes narrowed, anger striking sparks in them. "Instead of out doing a man's job? A woman's place is in the home, right?"

"I don't believe this is a man's world, Beth, but I do believe that the Customs Patrol is a man's job." She opened her mouth to interrupt, but Brand went on. "Women aren't accepted for combat duty in the army and, believe me, there isn't one job in the army that's any more dangerous than routine duty in the Patrol."

He stopped and she asked through tightly clenched teeth, "Are you through?"

"One more thing. I've known you for only a few weeks, Beth, but I've grown fond of you. And I respect you. If any woman can do this job, you can." His glance settled on her mouth. "But I wish you'd reconsider."

She was quiet while the waitress placed their food in front of them and watched the woman walk away before she looked back at Brand.

"Point taken. Ignored, but taken. Let's eat. Prejudice makes me hungry."

The food was good and she gave herself up to satisfying her appetite with the same gnawing questions unanswered. He had told her what he thought of women in the Patrol; he didn't want a female partner. Well, Beth thought maybe they should put Smitty and her together; we could look out for ourselves and let the big, strong men do the same.

Her lips twisted and the food suddenly stuck in her throat. Someone had not looked out for Jud.

"Finished?"

There was a mist in front of her as she met his eyes across the table, not speaking. They moved in silence toward the car.

"Feel like walking?" he asked.

She nodded and he eyed her sandals. "They'll be full of sand."

Stepping out of the network of straps on her feet, she bent and picked them up. "This will be better."

The uncertain anger inside her disappeared as she walked hand in hand with a man she hardly knew but found plenty to argue over with. He was the first man she had been this close to since Jud, a year ago. There was no feeling of betrayal because Brand was a fellow Customs Patrol Officer and when they graduated in a few days, they'd go their separate ways, likely never to see each other again. The thought wasn't too pleasant and she frowned, looking up into his shadowed face.

"Something wrong?" he asked.

"No." Her answer was short. He didn't want her serving with him; he thought she should have stayed in her safe classroom teaching languages to the kids, out of his way. Her fingers curled instinctively around his as they stood looking out across the water, quiet with the tide receding and the breakers out too far to be noisy.

Brand let go of her hand and draped his arm casually around her, his big hand resting at her waistline. She leaned against him, feeling his hard frame pressing into the lines of her body. He was well over six feet, making her seem small, especially since she was barefoot, her feet burrowed in the soft sand.

The hand on her waist tightened and he turned her toward him, one hand going beneath her chin to lift her face.

"No." Beth shook her head.

"This may be my last chance before graduation," he said.

"You don't have to kiss me at all."

"I want to," he countered, holding her so she couldn't pull away. She continued to look up at the wide unsmiling mouth. "All right, Beth?"

"Yes." Her voice came out a whisper and she pushed on tiptoes as much as she could in the deep sand. He helped by pulling her body upward and bending his head to hers. His mouth came closer and her hands, pressed against his chest to hold him away, dropped to his belt, thumbs hooking just inside. He hesitated before their lips met, his arms encircling her completely, imprisoning her slight form.

His mouth was cool as it touched hers, slightly damp and salty from the ocean breeze. With quiet insistence, he increased the pressure until her lips parted, accepting his kiss. His mouth didn't linger on hers but moved across her cheek to her ear, up to the pulse pounding in her temple, across her closed eyes, the tip of her nose and back to close over her lips, this time hard and demanding.

She whimpered, trying to pull away, but he just held her tightly. Her instinctive resistance vanished as her body responded to the feelings Brand was bringing alive. The tenseness eased from her body and she was drawn closer to him, feeling his shirt buttons digging into her breasts. One hand moved to the nape of her neck, fingers brushing the side of her throat, thumb against the nerve pumping below her ear. Their figures blended into one as his arms tightened.

The pressure on her mouth lessened as the tip of his tongue forced her lips further apart, and, for an instant, she allowed the intrusion, feeling the response even in her thighs. The hardness of his body against hers was a pleasant sensation as she recognized the fact that he wanted her. She gave in to the warm flow of ecstasy that his kiss gave her, letting her mouth stay warm and moist for him.

Realization that what happened next was up to her came through her fog, and twisting, she brought her arms down, thrusting away from him and he let her go. Neither spoke as, breathing hard, they stood close, her face turned to his. He brought his right hand up to touch her cheek then dropped it to his side.

"Beth?" It was as much a question as anything else, but she didn't dare answer him.

She stooped to pick up her sandals she had dropped and turned away. He caught her hand as they walked back toward the car, cupping his fingers over hers.

Fastening the seat belt around her, she was conscious of the feelings that lingered from their kisses. It was her first kiss since Jud had told her good-bye two weeks before he was killed; her first feelings of being alive since he had made love to her a year ago. She stared, unblinking, into the window on her side, Brandon Page's reflection was all she saw in the glass. Soon he too would be gone and she'd be on her own. Her hands, resting on each side of her, clenched into fists.

A big hand rested over the fist between them, pulling her fingers out straight, folding them inside his, and she could feel the roughness of callouses.

Turning her soft palm over to interlock her fingers with his, she asked, "What kind of job do you have in the Patrol that you have such hard callouses? I thought the thumb and trigger finger were all that got rough handling the guns."

He didn't answer for a long time, so long that she turned to look at him. He smiled as he met her glance. "Will you have a drink with me in my room if West isn't back yet?"

"What kind of an answer is that?"

Brand shrugged. "It wasn't an answer; it was a question."

"You have a plan to get me to change my mind about the Patrol?"

He smiled but only shook his head.

She said nothing more, sliding from the car as he opened the door in the parking area near their barracks. He linked his arm in hers and held it close to his side until they reached the door to his room. She waited as he unlocked the door, pushing it inward as he looked down at her. No one was inside.

Brand flipped the light switch and she stood in the

center of the room, looking around; the only difference between this room and the one she shared with Smitty was the apartment-sized refrigerator.

Her eyebrows went up. "How come?"

"We rented it." He walked past her, touching her arm and pointing to a straight chair between the two beds. "I don't have much of a selection. Brandy, plus a bottle of Chianti."

"Do you have any Seven-Up?"

"Well, yes, as a matter of fact, I do."

"I'll have one on the rocks, please."

He handed her a glass with bubbling liquid in it, poured a small amount of brandy in a glass for himself, pulling the other chair near her to sit down, stretching long legs out in front between them.

"When you leave here, do you catch a plane from Jacksonville back to Atlanta to get home?"

She laughed. "I catch a bus out of Brunswick to Atlanta, change buses there with a three-hour layover, then to Gainesville where my dad will met me. Dahlonega is twenty miles up the mountain from there."

He studied her face. "How far is it from Brunswick to Dahlonega?"

"About three hundred and thirty miles, give or take ten."

His eyes narrowed as he did some rapid calculating. "You'll be midnight getting home," he said.

She shook her head. "Probably three or four o'clock in the morning. The bus doesn't leave Brunswick till three thirty in the afternoon and that's if it's on time."

"How will your dad know when to pick you up?"

"I'll call him from Atlanta." She took a sip of her drink. "How long does it take you to drive to Nogales?"

"Three days, give or take a few hours." He smiled at her, leaning to place his glass on the table by her chair. "I have a suggestion."

"Yes?"

"I'll drive you home."

She gave him a look that said she thought he had lost his mind and gave voice to that thought. "You're crazy. Another day added to all that driving you already have to do? No, thanks. I don't want your untimely demise from overexhaustion on my conscience."

"It's not that far out of the way. I'll pick up Interstate 20 outside of Atlanta and head west."

"I'll take my chances on the bus," she told him.

"I'm going that away, anyhow," he said.

"How far that way?"

"To Dahlonega." He sat back watching her.

"Why?" Gray eyes narrowed, she tilted her head to one side, wondering what he had in mind.

"I'd like to meet your parents. I'm curious. Is your mother as pretty as you and does she have a southern drawl?"

In spite of herself, she laughed. "She's prettier."

He shook his head. "I doubt it." He picked his glass up from the table, looking into the amber liquid before he took a drink from it.

"Back to the subject of the Patrol, Beth."

Her head came up alertly, eyes fastened on him as he spoke. "Tell the truth, Beth. Whatever prompted you to join the Customs Patrol? Surely you don't feel you have to prove you're equal to men by doing something so out of character."

She went still, fingers tightening on the cool, moist glass in her hand. "Why do you think it's out of character for me?"

Deliberately, he let dark gray eyes go from her ash-blond hair, over the small breasts pushing against the gathered top, the tight jeans and bare feet stuck into sandals.

"A girl like you needs a man to look out for her, not vice versa," he said, his western accent more pronounced as he spoke slowly. "In the Patrol, it's a partnership." His eyes came back to meet hers and his voice was hard. "In a tight place, a man would put himself in danger to protect you and you know that. Perhaps you're counting on it."

Beth drew in her breath and let it out slowly, counting to ten, all the while her eyes holding his. She stood, placed the glass on the table, stepped across his legs stretched between his chair and the bed and looked back at him from the door.

"Whatever my reasons for joining the Patrol, I wasn't looking for protection."

"Wait, Beth, you asked—"

She swung the door open and said, "Good night, Mr. Page," stalking across the hall to her room, opening and closing the door quickly. Disappointment was keen within her, along with another feeling she couldn't identify.

He had let their earlier argument cool just enough to get her off guard, then he struck point-blank to get his feelings across. Shaking with anger, Beth went into her bathroom, taking the toothpaste to squeeze so violently that a long stream of the mess went all over the sink. She threw toothbrush and paste down in disgust, stopping only long enough to wipe up the goo before changing into lightweight pajamas and crawling into bed.

Hours later, she heard Smitty giggle outside the door, but when she entered the room, Beth pretended to be asleep.

THE NEXT DAY she sought out Don Genteel to ask when he thought assignments would come through. Outside his office, she hesitated as she heard Brand's voice.

"It's late in the course to be discussing this, Don," Brand was saying. "But all liberation aside, don't you think the department could use a little common sense about allowing women into the Patrol?"

The instructor smiled and shrugged. "Our government seldom makes use of logic and common sense, Brand. N.O.W. is rather powerful where government jobs are concerned."

"You'd think the danger in the patrol would be made doubly so should a male officer be overprotective toward a woman," he persisted.

"It's an individual assessment for each officer. You're right, though, in a way. It's not a fit place for a woman, but, then, it isn't fit for a man either. A world where decent people lose their lives over a few ounces of a chemical substance or anything else that will earn a few dollars is not a world fit for man or woman." After a moment, he went on. "If you're being specific about Beth Page, next to you, she's the best in the class."

Beth moved closer to allow her to see Brand as he

spoke. "Academically, yes, but it's different outside the classroom. The danger is real enough for me without my having to feel it necessary to protect a woman."

They had moved to the door and both of them looked up to see her, realizing she had heard the conversation. With a withering look at Brand, she turned on her heel and marched away, forgetting to ask about the assignment.

It was early afternoon, during break, so she headed for the cafeteria for a glass of iced tea. Perhaps that would cool off the steam raised by her eavesdropping. Unbidden, the memory of Brand's mouth on hers came and she drew in a sharp breath. Even his lovemaking was designed to get her to come around to his way of thinking. To convince her to give up the Patrol. Not a chance.

Chapter Three

Her throat still tight with anger, Beth made her way into the last class before exams, taking a seat about halfway up, looking around to see Smitty and Ted near the back. Smitty saluted and winked.

Anger and uncertainty, coupled with a strange sense of loss, had kept her awake until early morning. Thoughts of Jud and Brand mixed and she was more than a little conscious of the difference in the two men. Jud, gentle, determinedly protecting her; Brand, brash and determinedly trying to get her out of the Patrol.

"All right, Rice," Don Genteel was saying. "What would you do then?"

Beth had not heard the question but concentrated as Rice answered. "Attempted bribery of a Customs Officer must be reported to the United States attorney for prosecution under Section 201, Title 18, USC."

"Fine. If someone offers you *Mordida*, you put the bite on them instead. But suppose it's your partner, not you—what then?"

Rice looked confused. "Same rule, sir. No agent is exempt from any of the rules."

"I'm sorry, I didn't make myself very clear," Genteel said. "Consider this situation. Suppose you and your partner are on a stakeout. You're in the desert. Visibility is good. You and your partner are about one hundred yards apart, taking advantage of the only cover around. You see someone approaching in the distance, coming toward your partner. When he gets close your partner reveals himself. The stranger doesn't seem surprised. The two talk. You remain hidden as a precaution. That's just good procedure, but you watch the two closely. The stranger gives something to your partner who pockets it and goes back to his cover. The stranger continues on—away from the border into the United States. What action do you take?" Genteel looked over the classroom. "Somebody besides Rice."

His eyes narrowed as they met Beth's. "Page?"

She took a deep breath. "First, I'd..."

At the same time, Brand said, "It seems to me..."

Genteel gave a resigned sigh. He should be used to this by now. "*Miss* Page. What would your reaction be?"

"I'd stay at my post until we finished our assignment then I'd confront him with what I'd seen and ask the meaning of it."

"Suppose he told you it was none of your business?"

"I'd insist that it was my business."

"And if he still ignored you?"

Beth gave it another brief thought. "I'd report it to our supervisor."

Genteel nodded and looked at Brand. "Mr. Page. Any comments or additions?"

"I don't really care for her choice of words. You

don't *confront* your partner or *insist*. In our business you have to make decisions quickly and be especially fast at judging character. I would have known long before what type of man—pardon me—*person* my partner was, whether he would accept a bribe or not. If I *knew* he wouldn't accept a bribe, there would be no need to *confront* him. If you can't trust your partner, you may as well stay home."

Beth's lips tightened at his pointed statement.

The instructor looked around. "Any other comments?" No one said anything and he went on. "That's it for today."

Beth moved quickly out the side exit and down the hall, but Brand caught her arm as he cut her off, blocking her way.

"Beth."

Through clenched teeth, she said, "The instructor said that's all for today."

"Look, I know you're angry at me for what I said to Genteel and—"

"I underestimated you after all. You *do* know it all." She jerked away from him and walked away, cutting through the locker room to remove her fatigue uniform and replace it with a short jogging outfit.

She was, of course, the only one on the track. Everyone else was either studying or celebrating in advance, looking forward to leaving Glynco on Friday afternoon. She ran until her anger evaporated in the sweat that trickled down her body and then walked slowly to the room.

I shouldn't let him get to me, she decided. *After all, Brand only echoes my own doubts.* She lifted her head.

What he can't seem to get through his thick head is that no matter what he thinks, I'll see this job through at least one hitch. If it's for Jud or for me—it doesn't matter. I'm staying.

SMITTY LAY STRETCHED on the bed reading as Beth opened the door still breathing hard.

"It's ninety degrees out there and the humidity is ninety-five percent. And you're running in it. You really should know better, Beth."

She smiled at the girl who looked cool and rested. "I know, but that's the last run for me." Pushing her hair up off her neck, she slumped against the door. "I wish they'd give us our assignments."

"Oh, rumor has it they're not giving them out until after finals."

"That's great. Worrying about passing isn't enough. We have to worry about where we're going to get stuck, too."

Smitty grinned. "Makes sense to me. If you didn't like the assignment, you could flunk the final and get recycled into the next class."

Beth laughed. "My mind isn't that devious." She pulled the top of her jogging outfit over her head. "Are you hoping for Chicago?"

"Heck no, I'd rather have Hawaii or California. Any place I don't have to sleep with a hot water bottle."

"Smitty, with your looks, you won't ever have to worry about sleeping with a hot water bottle." She dodged the pillow Smitty threw at her.

"Okay, Miss Prim-and-Proper, where do you want to go?"

"Miami, preferably, but anywhere in Region Four will do."

Smitty groaned. "Heaven forbid. I can stand winters in Chicago better than summers in this oven."

"I'm used to it since I grew up here. I don't suppose you looked for the mail? I thought I'd have a letter from my parents."

"It still hadn't been put up when I went by there."

"I could dress and go check, I suppose," Beth said.

"Check mine while you're at it."

"Expecting anything?" she asked as she came out of the bathroom, slipping a Pink Panther T-shirt over her head and slipping on a pair of brief pink shorts.

"Anything for 'occupant' will do," Smitty said, returning to her book.

In the mail room Beth took several letters from her box, sifting through them as she turned. She drew in a sharp breath as she found a legal-sized official-looking envelope and ripped the edges in her hurry to open it. Maybe her orders...

Unfolding the letter, she scanned quickly down the page to see if there was a locality mentioned that might be her station and seeing nothing, went back to the greeting.

"Dear Brand: Let me congratulate you..."

She stopped in consternation, realizing she had opened a letter belonging to Brand. She turned it over and looked at the address: B. Page. Trying to get the letter back into the envelope was a problem after she had ripped it so badly in her hurry to get it open.

As much as she detested the idea, she would have to take the letter to him and explain why it was opened.

Outside Brand's room, she hesitated, then knocked lightly. The door opened immediately and she faced Brand. She handed the letter to him.

"I guess the clerk mixed us up. This is yours."

"It's been opened," he said unnecessarily.

"It was in my mailbox. I assumed it was for me and I opened it."

"Do you always treat your mail so roughly?"

"It's from Washington and looked official. I thought it might be my orders." Torn between the anger she still felt toward him and her obligation to apologize, she said, "Look, I'm sorry. I've never been around anyone with a name so like mine and I didn't think about it belonging to you."

"Join me for a drink?"

"What?"

"I asked if you'd like to join me for a drink."

"What—what for?"

He smiled. "We can celebrate getting my orders. I already knew but this makes it official. I never believe anything until it's written in black and white."

"Where are you going?"

"Nogales, Arizona, about a dozen miles from my home." He looked from the letter in his hand back at her. "You mean you didn't know that?"

"How would I know your assignment? I don't even know mine." She saw his glance at the letter and said angrily, "I didn't read that. As soon as I saw it was for you, I put it back in the envelope."

"Honesty. I like that in a partner."

"I'm not your partner," she told him.

He was smiling at her as she gave him a quizzical look. "What about that drink?"

"No, thanks, I'd better do some studying for the exams tomorrow."

"As good as your grades are, you can afford to take a night off."

"How do you know what my grades are?" she asked, curiosity getting the best of her.

"I listen to you in class. You not only know what you're talking about, you have the cutest southern drawl."

"You didn't agree with me the other day about the crooked partner."

"Okay. Let's say you usually know what you're talking about."

"Must you always be right in everything?"

"It helps."

She stared up at him a moment longer, aware that she wasn't as angry as she ought to be; she must be getting really tired.

"I'm sorry about the letter," she said and crossed the hall to her room closing the door as he stood watching her.

Smitty was in the bathroom already dressing to go out with Ted.

"No mail, Smitty," she told her.

"Would you like to go out with Ted and me tonight?" Smitty asked coming back into the room.

"Thanks, but no."

"I'm sure you'll be sorry."

"But you and Ted won't," Beth told her, grinning.

"You're right, of course, my friend. When we get our orders tomorrow, I may end up in New York where Ted's from and he'll be the one to get Hawaii. The government is so good at doing things like that." She looked straight at Beth. "Or I'll end up with the breakfast cereal out in the wide open spaces."

"Just hope you don't get Nogales, Arizona, wherever that is, because that's where our friend is going."

"How'd he rate his orders when no one else has theirs?"

Beth shrugged. "That's where he lives, too, so maybe that indicates we may all get our first choices."

"As Scarlett would say, tomorrow is time enough to worry about that." She touched Beth's shoulder as a knock sounded at the door and Ted called. "See you about sunup."

"Does your mother know you don't get enough sleep?" Beth called to her as she went out the door.

Left alone, Beth wandered over to the window overlooking the track she had run on the past several weeks, staying in shape for the rugged calisthenics Genteel's SS troops put them through. Her body was more slim than ever, not an ounce of flab lingering anywhere.

"I could outrun the bad guys," she murmured aloud. "But could I shoot them?" According to Genteel, when she found the answer to that question, it might be too late.

BETH AND SMITTY stood at the side of the classroom watching the other students talk among themselves.

Some nervous, some self-confident, all anxious to get the exams over with and scatter to the four winds.

Don Genteel strode into the room, nodding as they took their seats in front of him. Without a word, he went up and down the aisles, passing out the exam booklets.

"Grades for other qualifying areas of your exam will be posted with these. You have two hours for this written portion. When you finish, bring me your booklet, and in exchange you'll receive an envelope containing your assignment."

An audible sigh went around the room, then silence, as each one concentrated on the paper that meant so much. It had been a long twelve weeks.

Beth, among the first to finish her test, glanced at Smitty who gave her a "Well, shall we?" grimace and Beth nodded, gesturing "You first."

With a resigned look, Smitty walked to where Genteel stood, handed the blue booklet to him, and took the envelope he held with a murmured "thanks." She was busily ripping at the paper before she got to the exit.

Genteel looked up as Beth stopped in front of him. The stern countenance she had faced for weeks softened as he met her eyes.

"Beth? Funny, on official orders they usually put the full name. Shouldn't that be 'Elizabeth'?" he asked, smiling.

"My name is Beth, not Elizabeth."

"Just Beth." He looked at the letter again. "I'd better make sure you get the correct one. Good luck, Beth."

She thanked him, hurrying to catch Smitty standing in the hallway, staring in a dumbstruck pose at the piece of paper in her hands.

"Where, Smitty? Where are you going?"

"Region Two."

"Where's that?" Beth demanded.

"New York. Guess I'd better buy two hot water bottles. One for each foot." She drew in her breath as she turned to Beth. "What did you get?"

Beth held up the envelope. "I'm scared to look." She turned the letter sideways and ripped the end from it, drawing a sharp breath as she read the prominently displayed location.

"Don't let me die of suspense, Beth. Where?"

"Region Seven."

"Where's that?"

Beth choked on the next words. "Nogales, Arizona."

Neither of them spoke again as they turned toward the barracks building and their room. Once inside the room, they looked at each other for several seconds and Smitty opened her mouth to speak just as the knock came. She turned to open it and Ted stood on the other side.

He was grinning. "How far do I have to go AWOL to see you, honey?"

"The Big Apple, Ted. Since you're from New York, you must have gotten Timbuktoo."

A look of utter amazement wiped the grin from his face but only for a moment. He whooped as he crossed the threshold and picked Smitty up to whirl her around and around.

When he set her down, he pulled her close to squeeze her. "I got Region Two also."

The three of them exchanged disbelieving glances and all of them talked at once. As they settled down, Smitty turned to Beth. "Come out with us, Beth. We have something to celebrate whether you do or not." She grinned. "No hot water bottles; just drinks."

"I have to call my parents, Smitty. Have one for me."

The room was unbearably empty as the two happy graduates left her. She removed the hot fatigue uniform, showered quickly, and pulled on a pair of worn jeans and white cotton blouse. Picking up the assignment orders again, she sat on the side of the bed, still wondering at the reason she was sent so far from home when she knew the need for Patrol officers in the southeast.

She may as well get something to eat and call mother and dad, she thought. They would be disappointed to say the least.

Either she hadn't absorbed what had happened or she was numb, but it neither surprised her too much nor bothered her that she would be in Arizona. Maybe she'd be close to Brand, though the district in Nogales must be huge to take in such a lot of geography. She might be at one end and Brand at the other.

Dropping her keys into her bag, she opened the door just as Brand raised his hand to knock and they stared at each other in surprise.

Lowering his hand, he smiled, "How about that drink now? No more studying as an excuse."

She didn't move. "You knew, didn't you?"

"Knew?"

"My assignment. You knew mine as well as yours."

"Yes, I knew."

"You were hoping you could get me to change my mind, weren't you? Or else convince Washington they had made a mistake." He didn't deny it and she went on. "Did you work on them as hard as you did on me?"

"Harder."

"Tell me why are you so important that you got your assignment and knew mine before anyone else?"

"Let's get that drink and I'll explain."

"I'm almost curious enough to do just that."

"My car is outside."

She stared up at him for several seconds then turned to close the door behind them. Silently, they walked outside to the parking lot.

In the car he turned the air conditioning up high and they didn't talk as they drove toward the beach. Few cars were near the restaurant and cocktail lounge where they had eaten a few nights ago, and, inside, the cool dimness welcomed them.

"What would you like, Beth?" he asked as the hostess came to their booth.

"Seven-Up," she said still deep in thought.

"To celebrate?"

"I have a lot of thinking to do and I need a clear head for that."

He ordered a beer and turned back to her. "Thinking of asking for a change of assignment?"

"You mean change to another region?"

"No. Change from the Patrol to inspector or the administrative side. You'd still be able to do a needed job for Customs.''

"You really don't want a woman in your outfit, do you, Brand?"

"That's right." He leaned on the table. "I promised you the story about my assignment, Beth. I want you to listen to everything I say. It's just background for what will happen in the future in the area we'll be patrolling." He smiled. "And make no mistake about it—it's you and me. I'll be your supervisor and you will take orders from me without reservation."

She stared at him in shocked surprise. "You really meant it when you said I'd be your partner."

He nodded and waited as the waitress placed the Seven-Up in front of her and beer in front of him. "I was in the Patrol for several years until three years ago when I quit. For the job they want done, headquarters gives little backing, few officers, less money than is needed. After a few years, you stop fighting the organization. When I stopped fighting them, I got out."

He watched her as he went on. "Six months ago, gun-runners and drug smugglers came across the Mexico-U.S. border, cutting across the property adjoining mine. The owner was a friend of mine; we grew up together. They killed him."

Beth stiffened at the blunt, unexpected statement, but he went on. "The man who was my supervisor when I quit the Patrol is now a high-ranking official in Washington. He had been urging me to come back into the Patrol, but I decided I preferred ranching to the frustrations I knew so well. After Nash was killed, I called Washington and asked to go back in. That's what

I'm doing here—getting a refresher course to be sent back to Nogales to look for a way to prevent something like that happening there again."

Beth's fingers locked around the cool glass in front of her, but she didn't drink from it. Brand's eyes were black in the dimness of the room but they glinted with anger and she felt it directed at her.

"And you don't want me anywhere near you?"

"Look, Beth, we're talking about killers. People who count human life the way they do desert squirrels. Not only are smugglers running loose, we have the illegal drugs, illegal adoption rings, political kidnappings, and, if you remember the class about espionage, try thinking of the FALN camping on your doorstep."

Her head jerked. "The FALN? The terrorist group?"

He nodded. "They're moving our way and spreading along the southwestern border as well as the Gulf of Mexico."

She let that sink in before she sat back and looked at him. "I've been through the same training you have and with experience I'll make a good officer, Brand."

"You aren't listening, Beth. I know you'll be good at the job; I know you have incentive to do outstanding work; I know the organization says you can handle anything thrown at you, but neither of you knows what survival in the desert is like. Luxuries are something you read about in the magazines. You spend more time behind mesquite bushes and salt cedars than anywhere else."

He closed his eyes for a moment then said quietly enough to make her shiver, "Let me tell you, Beth, you turn right at Nogales, straight to hell."

The silence between them stretched out for several minutes when she said slowly, "But you love that land."

"It's my home, my people, Beth. Maybe I can't make everything better for them, but I could keep it from getting worse." His voice was quieter now. "You don't need to get into it, Beth. If you say the word, I can still get you a transfer, possibly back to Georgia or Florida."

"I don't need you to use your influence for me, Brand. I'll take the orders I have and make the best of them."

Angry dark eyes clashed with light gray ones asking for understanding.

He reached to lay a big hand on her arm as it lay on the table. "What can I say that would change your mind?"

Her gaze rested for a moment on his hand touching her arm then lifted to meet his eyes. "You could tell me the southwestern quarter of the United States has seceded from the Union and no longer came under the jurisdiction of the Treasury Department."

His fingers tightened almost painfully on her arm before he moved back in the booth. "You must have some damned stubborn ancestors."

"Probably related to yours."

They stared at each other and Beth's heart began a strange double beat as his mouth tightened but as she continued to look at him, he gave a resigned smile.

"Okay. If you're determined to stay, fill me in on the rest of your story. I know part of it...."

"No, you don't know anything about my story; you just think you do."

"I read your file. Several times."

"I read *Finnegans Wake* twice and never understood a word of it," she told him.

Ignoring her facetious comment, he went on. "You're twenty-seven; five feet six inches tall; weight?" He looked over the slender figure he could see above the table and, grinning, shook his head. "Master's degree in languages; taught three years in the Macon school system. Engaged to Judson Chambers, one of the best Customs Patrol Officers ever to walk the east coast when he was killed in the line of duty protecting several teammates."

"Stop it." After a year, it still shattered her thoughts.

"Would Jud have let you join the Patrol?"

"You go for the jugular, don't you?"

"My guerrilla training."

"I'm not a moon-chasing kid and I'm not looking for a protective arm around my shoulders. Just give me a chance."

"I never knew there were two syllables in chance. I'd love to hear you speak French with that accent."

Exaggerating her drawl even more, Beth said, "Y'all are in the South, Mr. Page. You must expect the natives to talk funny."

He put up his hand, laughing. "Shall we go?"

The sun had dropped behind a tall row of palms and a breeze blew away some of the daytime heat. Without asking, he turned her toward the beach and they walked to the edge of the water rolling in over the sandy strip. A freighter lay silhouetted against the darkening horizon, lights blinking.

He turned her slowly into his arms, holding her away

from him a moment before he pulled her up to kiss her. His fingers gently following her spine, moving downward to cup her curving buttocks, bringing her body to him. One hand tangled in the silvery waves of her hair, holding her head still to allow the kiss to go on.

Shimmering lights cruised the length of her legs where he had put one of his between them to support her. Pinwheels of fire spun out from his lips to hers, searing her, leaving her mindless with no thought of protest. It ended too soon and she gasped, still staring up into his unsmiling face.

"I'm still going," she whispered.

"This is a peaceful scene, Beth. You won't remember it in the weeks to come."

The cold facts of life thrown in her face helped her move away from him. She watched her feet go one in front of the other as they retraced their footsteps back to the car.

What would she remember in the weeks to come? Brand's hostility or his kisses? His determination to convince her she should transfer to another branch of Customs? His belief that the Patrol was no place for a woman?

All of them, she was sure. She would remember all of those things even if she forgot the tender scene by the peaceful waters of the Atlantic Ocean.

As he opened the door of the car and waited for her to slide in he barely touched her arm. A glance at his face showed that his thoughts were on something—or someone—else.

Few cars were in the parking lot as they got out and

walked side by side into the building. At her door, he said, "Are you planning to run tomorrow before roll call?"

"No."

"I'll see you at graduation, then, Beth. Good night." He kissed her cheek and waited until she was inside her room before he turned to open the door across the hall.

A glance at her watch showed it was too late to call her parents. She should have remembered it before now. A wry grin parted her lips and the movement reminded her of Brand's heart-stopping kiss on the beach.

In bed her thoughts turned to Jud. Laughing, fun-loving Jud, whose tenderness had turned her into a woman capable of feeling and giving love. Her world had been contained within the circles of love for Jud and her parents, a job she enjoyed, and friends. That world had been smashed with his death and she hadn't yet been able to fit the ends of the circle back together.

I can't take his place, not the way Brand thinks I'm trying to do. But surely my efforts won't be entirely wasted.

And Brand. She smiled with satisfaction. He didn't get his way, after all, and would have to accept a female partner. Not partner, per se; he was the supervisor and she had no doubt that he would expect more from her than from her counterparts.

THE FIELD of fifty navy blue clad officers of the United States Customs Patrol Class Number 200 stood at attention as diplomas were handed out. By nine thirty, they were dismissed and the students scattered for individual destinations.

"We have to catch the bus into Jacksonville in thirty

minutes, Beth. What time does your bus leave?''
Smitty's dark eyes shone with excitement. Her assignment had turned out about a thousand percent better
than she could have expected and she sympathized
with Beth having to be stationed with Brand Page.

"Not till three thirty. I have enough time to relax
before I go."

Smitty stood in front of her. "I'm going to miss you.
Will you write?"

"Of course. Unless I'm stationed behind a tumbleweed and forgotten."

Ted picked that time to knock on the door and in a
flurry of good-byes, they were gone.

Somehow, she expected the second knock and opened
the door to Brand.

"Congratulations," he said.

"For what?"

He raised thick eyebrows. "You didn't know?"

She shrugged and motioned him inside the room,
closing the door to lean against it. "I won the prize for
being the most stubborn Page in your book?"

He grinned. "That too." He touched her cheek,
brushing a heavy wave back. "You were second highest
in scholastic standing."

"Behind you."

"Yes." When she made no comment, he went on,
"Didn't you look at the piece of paper you got with the
diploma?"

She shook her head, glancing toward the dresser
where two rolled-up articles lay but made no move to
see what he was talking about. "If it doesn't impress
you, it won't help me a bit."

"Oh, but it does impress me. You'd make an out-standing career diplomatic officer in Washington."

She laughed. "No sale, Brand. You're stuck with me."

He shrugged. "I thought as much. Well, let's get started toward Dahlonega so we'll get home before dark."

"I'm taking the bus."

"Have you already bought your ticket?"

"No, but—"

"Then we don't have to return it," he said logically.

"First you do all you can to get rid of me then you want to drive me home." She cocked her head to one side, pursing her lips. "Let me guess. You want to talk my parents into having me committed. Grounds? Anyone who would take a job standing behind a mesquite bush in the desert under a broiling sun just to arrest someone who will be back on the street before you can take a shower has to be crazy."

"Don't they?"

She walked around him to sit on the edge of the bed. "Yes, but I'm going to do it anyway. Don't bother my parents."

Brand folded his arms across his chest and rocked back on the heels of well-polished cowboy boots. "If you refuse to ride with me, I'll follow you to the bus station carrying a sign that says: 'Beth Page unfair to Brand Page. I want equal rights.' Everyone will think we're married and had a lovers' quarrel. I'll bet I'd get more sympathy than you."

"Just tell me why, Brand."

"It's a chance to get to know my new partner before

we have to serve in the field together. Knowing your partner is the best way to stay alive."

"You could be right. I guess we could put you up for the night. You'd get to taste mother's cooking and dad's wine." She had been making circles on the bedspread with her forefinger and now looked up at him.

"You really would do it, wouldn't you? Follow me with that sign?"

"I always do whatever it takes to get a job done."

Chapter Four

They didn't get to know each other well in the six or so hours it took to drive from Brunswick to Dahlonega. They discussed everything from politics to the latest ridiculous fashions to the changes in the weather and whether they were caused by moon shots or volcanoes. No problems were solved even when they ended up in a heated dispute over cause and effect.

They were leaving the small café outside of Gainesville where Beth told him the barbecue was the best in fifty states when Brand suddenly asked, "Would Jud really want you to do this?"

Beth, in the process of fastening her seat belt, turned to face him and he saw the color drain from her face and the pupils dilate to take in almost all of the light gray color of her eyes. Her lips parted and the tip of her tongue touched where the indentation in the top lip formed a cupid's bow above the full lower one.

The subject of Jud had been studiously avoided as if by mutual consent until now. Before she answered him, her gaze went from his dark hair, over his tanned face, past the mouth that had been the only one to touch hers since Jud's, and back to dark gray eyes waiting for her to speak.

"Yes." The single word softly spoken was not what he wanted to hear. He touched her cheek with one finger and turned to start the car. It was somehow a caring touch, unbelievably tender.

"You turn left at the first stoplight," she said as he pulled from the parking lot. Thinking about his abrupt question, Beth stared unseeingly through the window. It was as though he understood her belief even while disagreeing with her.

The road began to climb gradually as soon as they left the main highway and the sun dropped ahead of them as they drove west toward Dahlonega. Brand handled the small car expertly, rounding curves and climbing hills until they came upon the city limits with a sign that read Dahlonega, pop. 2856—elev. 2126 feet.

"Big city," he said and grinned at her. "Compared to Patagonia, I mean."

"Do you count the cows in Patagonia?"

"They don't allow them inside the city limits, but even so we have about a thousand people. Scattered around the mountains and desert, of course." He thought a moment. "I always suspected they counted several times to come up with that many people."

The neatly kept houses sitting near the street already had lights burning as the early dusk settled. Down the main street, a few people strolled, in no apparent hurry to get anywhere.

"That's the new Postal Service building where mother works," Beth pointed out. "Turn right at the next light."

"Where does your dad work?"

"He runs a dairy farm."

"You're the only child?"

"Not exactly a child, but yes, the only one."

"Small family," he commented after a moment.
"Do you have brothers and sisters?"

"Just me."

"And your parents?"

He shook his head. "They died several years ago."

"You *really* are a small family."

They drove over a cattle guard and Beth told him,
"This is where our property begins."

Ahead of them the road turned and as they rounded
the curve and up a slight incline, they could see the
house sprawled beneath big oak trees, lights in several
rooms and on the wide porch that went across the entire front of the house.

As they stopped in front of the steps Beth indicated,
the screen door opened and a tall, broad-shouldered
man ran down the brick steps. A shock of silver-gray
hair very nearly the color of Beth's was enough to
identify him as her dad. She slid from the car into his
arms.

He held her without a word until she pulled away and
turned. "This is Brand, Dad. He was kind enough to
bring me home." She made a face at Brand as she said
it and he grinned.

"Saved me a few hours sleep, Brand. Thanks. I'm
Jim Page." He extended his hand.

"A pleasure, sir," Brand said and they shook hands.
He turned to open the trunk of the car for their luggage
as Beth's mother came out on the porch.

Beth ran up the steps to be caught up in a tight hug. "Hi, Mother."

"Oh, Beth, you've lost weight. But you look good."

Introductions over, they sat in the high-ceilinged living room, its walls covered in white wallpaper sprinkled with tiny blue flowers. Heavy furniture covered in navy-blue figured material was set in a comfortable arrangement facing a wide stone fireplace.

"Drink, Brand?" her dad asked.

"Bourbon and water?"

Jim nodded. "I have some scuppernong wine I saved for Beth and Mary Ann," he told him as he handed the glass to Brand.

"Scuppernong?" He grinned at Beth as Jim's drawl drew the word out.

"Brand needs to be educated in that respect, Dad. I'm sure scuppernongs don't grow in Nogales."

A flicker touched Brand's face and was gone as he agreed. "I've never heard of them."

Jim explained the origin of the wild white grapes as he poured light liquid in two glasses, handing them to Mary Ann and Beth. "Beth used to help me gather them. I always let her climb the trees and shake the vines." He grinned at his daughter.

"I'd like to have seen that. Although she's still quite adept at climbing ropes."

"Oh?"

"He's referring to the monkeyshines they put us through at the Academy. Over walls and bars and swinging through the air. I can't help it if they put me in with the older group who had a hard time keeping up."

The talk finally got around to the Patrol and Beth saw

questions in Jim's eyes, but she knew once they started discussing where she was going to be stationed, it would be argument time. She was too tired to defend herself against Brand and explain why she was being stationed in Arizona to her parents. She yawned.

"Oh, Beth, of course you're tired. Your rooms are ready any time."

"I am tired," Beth told her. "Brand?"

"If Jim isn't quite ready for bed, I'll stay up. Good night, Beth."

Mary Ann followed her up the curving stairway to her room at the east side of the house. The door was open and she stood a moment looking at the familiar room that had been hers for fifteen years, since the original old home was remodeled and the upstairs added. White organdy Priscilla curtains hung at the wide windows, as fresh and pretty as the day they were first put there.

She turned to smile at her mother. "It's good to be home."

Mary Ann sat on the bed. "Is Brand more than a friend, Beth?"

She hesitated before answering then said slowly, watching her mother's expression, "He isn't even a friend, Mother. We can barely be civil to each other for five minutes. He disapproves of women in the Patrol and am sure he's telling Dad right now that he shouldn't allow me to stay. Smitty and I put up with a good deal of prejudice since we were the only two women in the class."

Mary Ann was familiar with her class at the Academy through Beth's regular letters that told her everything about the people she met and nothing of their training.

"He doesn't want you in the Patrol because you're a woman or because he's afraid for you?"

Beth stared. Her mother was smart. "I don't know, but whatever his reason, it isn't enough. I'm staying."

Mary Ann nodded and stood up. "We'll have time to talk later, honey. You'd better get some sleep."

"Mother." At the tone of Beth's voice, she turned. "I didn't get Region Four as I'd hoped. I'll be stationed in Nogales, Arizona."

"Arizona? But why? I thought—"

"So did I, Mother, but I'll be stationed with Brand. That's why he's so determined I should ask for a transfer, so I'll be out of his outfit."

"Does Jim know?"

"Probably by now he does. Brand has given him a very prejudiced point of view, I'm sure." She crossed the room to hug her mother. "Don't worry. After a year, I can ask for a transfer back to this area and if I do good work, who knows, they may even give it to me."

As Mary Ann left, closing the door behind her, Beth undressed and walked to the window to look out over the darkness toward the dairy barns. She could smell the hay and the ever-present odor of cows that had never been unpleasant to her. The smell of hyacinths and jasmine came through the open window.

Turning away, she slid between the cool sheets and was asleep almost instantly, not even hearing Brand's footsteps as he came up the stairs a few minutes later.

THE SOUND of the old rooster crowing beneath her window woke Beth and she smiled without opening her eyes. A moist breeze came through the window and she breathed deeply of the familiar fragrances. The house was quiet, but she was sure Mary Ann and Jim were already downstairs even though it was barely daybreak. Mornings, even Saturday mornings, came early for a dairy farmer.

She opened her eyes as a soft knock came at the door. "It's open. Come in," she called, smiling, expecting to see Mary Ann.

Brand pushed the door open and stood just inside. "What are you doing up so early?" she asked in surprise, raising up on her elbow, almost forgetting she wore nothing beneath the sheets.

"Habit," he said quietly, his eyes following the length of her clearly outlined body under the thin cover.

He pushed the door closed and walked to the bed to stand looking down at her, watching her eyes widen as he neared. He stooped beside her and rested his hand on the sheet over her waist, his thumb caressing across the flatness to her navel. As his mouth covered hers, still warm with sleep, his hand moved over the curve of her hip, hesitating before coming back to cup her breast.

The sound she made could have come from surprise or from the warmth of the unexpected thrill that slid in a slow, sensual path from her lips to her thighs.

Beneath the pressure of his mouth, her head lowered to the pillow and her hands rested on his shoulders. His lips moved gently across hers, following her cheekbone to her throat, touching the rapidly beating pulse, to the hollow at the base.

"Brand," she whispered as his head lifted. She stared up into eyes hidden beneath stubby lashes.

"Remind me to tell you to always lock your doors, Beth," he said as he stood up. "It's a dangerous practice in Arizona to leave them open." He smiled at her. "Perhaps in Dahlonega, too." He turned to leave. "I smell coffee."

She didn't answer as he left, closing the door behind him.

He's trying to maneuver me, she thought. *He's trying to tell me you can get close to people who can hurt and be hurt. Again.* She quivered at the remembered touch of his hands, the sweetness of the unexpected kiss—and ignored his intended warning.

Shivering, not from cold, she got up and dressed, running lightly down the steps to join them in the big old-fashioned kitchen, built to be a functionally working kitchen. The three of them sat at a heavy round pine table and she kissed the top of Jim's head as she slid in the chair beside him where Mary Ann had poured her a cup of coffee.

"Stay for the weekend, Brand," Jim said. "There's a few activities planned for the Labor Day holiday and Beth can always take you fishing."

Brand looked at Beth to find her light gray eyes on him. "Or panning for gold," she said, smiling at him.

He gave her a disbelieving look. "Gold?"

She nodded. "At one time, prior to the Civil War, Dahlonega was a rip-roaring, wide-open mining town with all the symptoms of the period. Saloons, gambling houses, desperadoes, and duels. The war came and, after that, what might be termed civilization. The big veins of gold ran out, but people still go in and pan, mostly for recreation, not much profit.''

"You know how to do this, of course?" Brand's question showed his doubts.

"Of course." She put her cup down and for a moment thought of the gold bands Jud had made for them from the fruits of one whole weekend of labor in the mountain streams. They had been put away with all her memories of him. She straightened.

"Stay and we'll check out some of the places I know about that few tourists ever find," she promised.

"Sounds like fun," he said, and at the drawn out western drawl in his voice, Beth wasn't so sure he meant just that.

One of Mary Ann's fabulous breakfasts behind them, Jim brought the cooler from the garage, one she and Jud had used hundreds of times.

Maybe Arizona's a good place for me to go. I won't be seeing Jud every time I turn around.

"There's plenty of biscuits left, Beth, and how about the fried chicken left from yesterday?"

"Great, Mother. I don't suppose you made peanut butter cookies?"

Her mother's soft laughter answered for her and she reached for the gingerbread-house ceramic cookie jar to get a dozen cookies, wrapping them in foil—after popping one in her mouth.

"Dad got any wine left, Mother?" she asked as she finished packing the food.

"I don't know if he and Roger left any or not, Beth. Check in the basement."

Roger was Dahlonega's police chief and he and his wife, Edie, were close friends from since before Beth was born. She smiled as she ran down the steps, looking closely at the shelves of cans and jars from the summer fruits and vegetables.

Over the chest-type freezer were several jars and she selected a quart-sized one, looking on the label to read: Scup. wine, 1979. Wow! How did Dad and Roger miss that one?

Taking a bag of ice from the freezer, she ran back up the steps with her prize, placing the jar of wine in the bottom of the cooler and emptied the ice on top of it.

"Are we staying a week?" Brand asked from behind her.

"It's a thought," she said, smiling.

"Your dad gave me the fishing rods and rubber boots. He said you'd know what else to take."

"We'll get the pans from the shed as we pick up the jeep. Lend a hand."

They moved the cooler to the back porch and she said, "Okay. Now for the pans and the jeep and we're ready."

Jim had opened the garage where the jeep was kept and she went past it to the back wall where several shelves held all sorts of farm equipment. She lifted two of the circular pans, handing one to Brand. A wire mesh, used to strain the water, covered half of the pan. She held hers up to the light, pointing to the minute specks of dull yellow.

"Part of my last haul," she told him, turning to the

jeep to climb in, placing the pan behind the driver's seat. "Ready?"

He swung up in the seat, and Beth backed out and pulled up to the porch where they had left the cooler. They loaded it and then Beth turned to wave at Mary Ann who stood in the doorway.

Driving through the thick growth of pines on a road no more than two jeep tracks wide, Beth said, "We'll go by Dockery Lake. It's probably crowded but it's pretty and we can go to Cooper Creek and the Moccasin that way."

"Is that where we get rich?"

She laughed. "You sound skeptical." She shook her head. "Where's your sense of adventure? It's a holiday, we have a delicious lunch packed, and not a care in the world—especially after we finish the jar of scuppernong wine I snitched from the basement."

She was laughing as she went on. "I guess I have to learn to live without scuppernongs in Arizona since they need water to grow and you say there isn't much."

Glancing across at him, she froze at the expression on his face. His mouth was a straight line, eyes dark and narrowed as they met hers.

"It's not the only thing you'll do without, Beth. Remember that."

Her hands tightened on the wheel and she put the brakes on, rolling to a stop. "I want this job and I'm willing to do without whatever I must," she said, turning toward him. "Am I going to have to fight you all the way, Brand? Am I not going to get the chance to make it on my own?"

"It's not the job for you, Beth. It's rough; the people

are rough; there's no southern graciousness in the desert, just the fight for survival. Our assignment will be the western half of the sector and I'll warn you once more, Beth, you turn right at Nogales, straight to hell.''

He was hunched forward in the seat, staring at the forest to his right. He turned back to her. "I'm thinking of you.''

She started the jeep again and concentrated on the turns and twists of the trail she followed. They came to a two-lane blacktop and she pulled onto it, turning right. "If it's because I'm a woman, Brand, pretend I'm a man and treat me accordingly.''

He laughed softly. "I don't have that much imagination." He took a deep breath. "I'll get you any job you want as close to Dahlonega as I can if you'll get out of the Patrol.''

"No." She sighed. "I don't think we're going to enjoy our trip. Do you want to go back?''

After a moment of dead silence, he said, "We'll forget shop talk. I won't ruin the day for you.''

The conversation about the Patrol started the uneasiness again and she tried to put it out of her mind. Reporting day was still two weeks and two days away and the long holiday weekend was here to enjoy.

She slowed as they approached a sign for Dockery Lake, with an arrow pointing straight ahead. She followed the arrow into a sandy lane around a tall clump of hackberry bushes, and the dark water spread out in front of them.

"Not too crowded," Beth said in surprise.

"Maybe everyone decided to be lazy today.''

"The main camping and fishing area is on the other

side." She squinted at the sky, the sun hidden for the moment by puffy white clouds. "Let's take a canoe out and try our luck."

The canoes were rented on a strict honor system. A tin can fastened to the side of a wooden slat used as a seat had a hand-printed sign: "Please deposit $1.00 for use of the canoe."

"How long can we keep it for a dollar?" Brand asked, taking one from his pocket and depositng it in the can.

"All day if we want it." She reached into the back-seat of the jeep for the rods. As she handed one to him, she said, "You'll need a hat to keep the gnats and mos-quitoes away from your head and face."

He took the straw hat without comment and grinned as she slapped an army camouflaged campaign hat on the back of her head. Together they pushed the canoe into the edge of the water, climbed into it, and shoved off with the oars. She pointed to a spot off to her right and he helped her turn the canoe and stopped paddling as she placed her oar at her feet. The wind blew at a pleasant five miles per hour across the lake as they baited the hooks and threw their lines in.

Beth settled against the slat she had been sitting on, tilting the hat over her eyes. Brand still sat on the cross-seat, straw hat pushed to the back of his head, eyes resting on the lines they held. She studied him, wondering why he wasn't married. He was nice enough looking, but perhaps he didn't want women around him on or off the job.

"If you caught one, could you take him off your hook?" he asked, interrupting her musings.

"I don't know," she said, her voice lazy and uncaring. "I've never caught any."

He turned to look at her and she watched his expression from beneath the floppy brim of her hat, surprised to see him smile as his glance traveled her jeans-clad figure to her bare feet and her eyes widened as he leaned over to kiss her big toe. He bit gently into the pink flesh.

"Bare toes are sexy," he said, straightening to look back at the fishing lines.

She lay still, startled at feelings his casual touch stirred in her and, unbidden, the memory of his gentle caresses early that morning returned to send a warm thrill through her body.

"Hey, look," he said and Beth sat up to see his line moving away from the canoe. He played it out, letting it go for several feet, then started pulling it in. The line left the water with a three-inch perch wiggling on the hook.

"We'll invite company for dinner," she said, awe in her voice as he caught the fish and worked it loose, releasing it back into the water.

He glared. "Cynic. At least, I caught something."

"With all that success gone to your head, shall we try our luck with the gold? We could be millionaires by nightfall."

"Your parents could be minus a smart-mouthed daughter by night," Brand threatened.

Beth grinned as they turned back to the shore, securing the canoe as they had found it.

"Let's eat now," she suggested.

He nodded in agreement and they put the dishes

from the cooler on one of the tables in the shade of the water oak trees.

"Looks good. Even after Mary Ann's farmer-sized breakfast, I'm hungry."

"It took a lot of energy to pull in that prize catch," she told him.

"I get even, eventually," he promised her.

She laughed, handing him a Styrofoam cup half filled with light burgundy liquid.

"Only half a glass of the famous scuppernong wine?" he asked.

"You may not like it and I don't want to waste it if you don't."

Brand tilted the cup, taking a big swallow of the wine, concentrating as he measured the taste. He nodded, handing her his cup again. "I promise not to waste a drop."

The drone of bees in the late summer sun was the only sound above the whisper of the leaves moving in the slight breeze.

"Mexico has the right idea."

"About what?"

"Siesta time. That's when you eat too much and get lazy and sleepy."

"I agree. There's a blanket in the jeep."

A few minutes later with the food back in the cooler and the blanket spread in the shade, they stretched out a few feet apart. Beth lay on her stomach, head pillowed on her arms. Brand lay on his back, hat covering his face, hands clasped behind his head.

Through lowered lashes, she regarded the still figure, wishing they could have had a better start with their acquaintance since it was going to be an extended one—due to her stubbornness, Brand would tell her.

Why did the government have to complicate things by sending her where she'd be the only female with a supervisor who disliked her and made no secret of it?

Idly, she watched a huge black-winged mosquito hover momentarily and settle on the hard muscle of his arm. She sat up quickly and swung, the flat of her hand smacking against his flesh and was caught tightly in his arms as he rolled over on her, his hat knocked from his face.

Staring into his narrowed eyes, she said, "I only..."

His mouth was hard on hers, tasting of the sweet wine still there. He held her arms pinned beneath his, one hand turning her head to give him full access to her lips. His head moved, tormenting her as his mouth moved back and forth, parting to let his teeth nip into her full lower lip.

She gasped as he raised his head. "You should never strike without provocation," he said, his voice as hard as his kiss.

"I'm sorry." She stared wide-eyed at him. "Mosquito bites here are very potent and I thought if I waited to warn you, it would bite and fly away before you could kill it."

"A mosquito?"

She moved her arms, pushing his right one up so that he could see the bright smear and opened her hand to show the remains of the insect and his blood.

His gaze went from her strong evidence back to meet her gray eyes. "Looks like I owe you an apology."

Instead of releasing her, he lowered his face, gently

kissing her eyelids until they closed, moving down her cheek, brushing across her mouth, coming back to settle on her lips, whispering against them. Her lips parted and her hands went to his shoulders, her body moving in a slow caress beneath him.

After a long moment as their bodies recognized each other's demands, he said softly, "You know better than that."

"Yes," she whispered, aware of the hardness of his body against her thighs.

He held her an instant longer, sat up and pulled her with him. "Let's go seek our fortune."

Neither spoke as she drove away from the lake, turning southwest on a narrow gravel road.

She broke the silence. "We're just off the Appalachian Trail at the foot of the Blue Ridge Mountains," she said. "This takes us by Cooper Creek and Cane Creek Falls."

Cottonwood trees became thicker as the road followed a creek bank, and at an open space Beth turned off to park.

"Those boots fit you?" she asked.

"More or less."

She nodded. "Wear them." She pulled on a pair that went nearly to her thighs.

"Why?"

"Besides giant, economy-sized mosquitoes, we have a few water moccasins around this time of year."

"I thought you said Cooper Creek; not Moccasin," he reminded her.

"Our snakes are illiterate."

"What do you mean?"

She smiled over her shoulder. "They can't read the signs."

Behind her, he snorted and muttered words she was sure wouldn't be complimentary if she had understood him. Ignoring his comments, she handed him one of the pans. "We'll walk up a little way where the water's shallow and runs across rocks and sand. It's easier to see that way."

Beth selected a spot and stooped to put her pan under the water, using one hand to scoop sand from the creek bed. Pulling it up, she slushed the murky liquid till most of the water drained out and turned around.

"See?" In the silt remaining in the pan, bright flecks winked at them.

"Are we rich?" he asked, bending closer.

She dumped the speckled sand into the flat oblong box she carried and scooped up another panful. "We'll try a few more times before we cash all this in."

Brand followed her example and soon they were carrying half a box of sand. "What do we do now?" he asked.

"Take it home to Dad and let him run it through the gold box and extract anything of value."

"We have all the fun and he does the work."

"I believe in letting the experts do the job." She sat down to strip off the wet boots and glanced at the sun dropping behind the thick trees. "What do you say we skip Moccasin Creek and make it home in time for supper?"

He agreed and they climbed back into the jeep. As she guided it along the narrow road, he looked around.

"It's different," he said. She turned to look at him

and he gave her a brief glance. "We don't have thick forests like this."

She stiffened, waiting for his next statement she knew would sting, but he remained quiet, looking straight ahead. She concentrated on driving, wondering how they would survive on the isolated patrols he described in Nogales. He would always be stressing their differences.

They came to a narrow bridge and she pointed. "Those are the falls I mentioned." A frothing cascade of water plummeted fifteen feet into a dark pool then ran smoothly under the bridge where she had stopped. After a moment of watching the cool looking scene, she bumped on across the bridge, turning onto the sandy trail they had followed that morning.

Their day's trip had taken them in a circle ending several miles from the house. She broke the silence just before they reached home.

"There isn't much entertainment around Dahlonega, Brand, but Mother and Dad are going to the VFW dance tonight if you'd like to go."

When he didn't answer right away, she glanced at him to meet his appraising stare. "At a dance, I can hold you without any excuse."

"Why, yes, I suppose you can," Beth said.

"Good." Brand turned back to look at the road.

A few minutes of strained silence later they turned into the driveway and she pulled the jeep around to the back of the house to park near the shed where they had taken their equipment from that morning.

"Any luck?" Jim asked, coming around the building toward them.

"The only thing biting today was mosquitoes," Beth said, her glance meeting Brand's. "Brand caught our limit of perch at Dockery Lake and we found a fraction of an ounce of yellow stuff that might be gold." Jim helped Brand lift the cooler from the jeep as Beth put the fishing poles across the beams along the wall.

Jim turned the nuggets Brand gave him over in his hand as they went toward the house. "Supper's about ready. Mary Ann figured you'd be back in time to eat."

"We're starved," Beth told him.

Mary Ann met them on the porch, smiling as she wrinkled her nose at Beth. "I think you have time for a shower," she said, taking in Beth's smudged face and dusty jeans.

Thirty minutes later they were at the dining table and Jim was passing a steaming bowl of chicken and dumplings to Brand. He glanced at Beth to see her grin.

"The peach cobbler is even more fattening. Mother doesn't know how to cook any other way," Beth said.

Brand shook his head, taking a generous helping from the bowl. "Two thousand miles is a good distance between me and your cooking, Mary Ann," he said.

When the peach cobbler with heaps of whipped cream was passed to him, Brand said, "We walked ten miles today but not enough for this."

"We can go to the dance tonight and work off a few calories," Jim said.

"If Brand wants to," Beth said.

"Sure," he said, his eyes meeting hers, reminding her of his statement: *I can hold you without any excuse.*

As they cleaned the table, Mary Ann asked, "Any

problems with Brand trying to talk you out of the Patrol?''

Beth shook her head. "We did fine, but for how long, I don't know. I always wondered what an armed truce was. Now I know, or at least that's what it feels like. I'm waiting for the blow to fall."

"Maybe he gave up," Mary Ann said, hopefully.

"No, Mother, he isn't the kind, believe me." She turned to see her mother's concerned look and smiled. "It'll be all right when I get into the assignment. I'll stay out of his way."

Leaving her mother, she went to look for something suitable to wear to the dance. Jeans would do, but she felt like dressing up and pulled out a print cotton dress with cool green sprigs on white. Short cap sleeves, tight-waisted with a full-length gathered skirt, its bodice hugged her slender figure. The sweetheart neckline curved just above the swell of her breasts. She hunted until she found sandals suitable for a waltz or a rowdy Cotton-Eyed Joe, either of which the band at the VFW could handle with equal ability.

As she went down the stairs, Jim and Brand were standing near the fireplace, each holding a drink. Brand was handsome in white shirt and light blue pants. They turned to look at her as she swung down the last few stair steps.

Jim smiled and winked at her. Brand's expression closed as he watched her walk toward them and she felt a moment of uncertainty.

I'm paranoid about him, she thought, and mentally shrugged away her misgivings, stopping near Jim as Mary Ann joined them.

"Two beautiful ladies for us to escort, Brand. Shall we go?"

The VFW wasn't far from the outskirts of town and in a few minutes they pulled into an already crowded parking lot.

"Roger and Edie promised to save us seats at their table," Mary Ann said as they walked into the building.

"There they are," Jim said, threading his way through the crowd, pulling Mary Ann behind him with Beth following, her arm linked with Brand's, conscious of the hard muscle against her ribs.

She held onto him in the flurry and confusion of introductions and, even with all the handshaking, he stayed close, glancing at her occasionally with a half grin.

All of Dahlonega seemed to be at the dance and everyone knew the Pages. During a break of the hugs and "Where have you beens?" directed at Beth, Brand took her arm, pulling her onto the dance floor. The band was playing a smooth ballad and she went into the circle of his arms, moving easily with his expert lead.

He was looking down at her as she looked up and she shook her head at the expression she read in his eyes. "Don't say it."

"What?"

"That I'd better enjoy tonight because I can't wear dresses like this chasing desert squirrels and jackrabbits."

His arms tightened as he continued to look down at her. "Enjoy it, Beth. There won't be many nights like this."

They danced in silence as she wondered about the

man who held her and his determination to keep her
from going to Nogales. *Well, I didn't ask for Nogales; it's
his precious organization that's sending me out there. Let
him argue with them about it.*

The noise of the crowd faded away as she moved automatically with Brand and for some reason, her thoughts
went to Smitty. Happy, fun-loving Smitty who thought
Brand belonged in the wide-open spaces—and she was
right, of course.

She smiled at him and he stopped dancing to lead her
through an open door onto a porch, keeping her hand
in his as they went down two steps onto the lawn. A
lighted fountain threw shadows across them as she followed him over the grassy carpet into the shadows of a
line of cedars.

He turned abruptly and she bumped into him. With a
swift movement, he pulled her to him and, as she lifted
her face, his lips met hers in a gentle kiss that surprised
her. She was expecting roughness, a kiss that would
show her that all would not be sweetness where they
were going. He lifted his head, still holding her, his
eyes hidden by stubby lashes.

"Did you love him very much?" he asked quietly.

She stared up into his face and realized her arms
were around his neck and, on tiptoe, her body pressed
to the hardness of his.

"Yes. Very much."

He continued to look down at her, then slowly took
his arms away from her, reaching up to capture her
hands and bring them down in front of him. He kissed
her fingers and turned back toward the hall, tucking
her hand under his arm.

They walked in silence back across the lawn to the steps and stood aside as another couple came through the door. He caught the door, letting her pass through in front of him, walking alongside her to casually place his arm around her waist as they made their way back to the table.

THE DANCE ENDED at one o'clock and by one thirty the four of them were lounging comfortably around the big living room. Beth sat on the couch beside Brand, her head tilted over the back, half-closed eyes on the sparkling white of the ceiling. Her lips still tingled from Brand's brief kiss, her fingers alive where his mouth lingered. Wonder filled her that, after a year, she enjoyed being touched again. Her heart was healing.

Beside her Brand stirred and she turned to smile at him as he stood up and walked away from her to stand by the mantel. "I'll be leaving early in the morning and I have to talk to all of you before I go." He smiled briefly. "I really have enjoyed it here."

He hesitated as his glance went from Mary Ann to Jim. "Beth has been assigned to my outfit in Nogales, Arizona. That's home to me; a foreign country to anyone else who's never lived in the desert. It's not quite as wild as it was at the turn of the century, but it's just as dangerous, perhaps more so."

Beth sat up straight, head lifted as she listened. "I don't want Beth there. It isn't personal; it's a matter of survival, mine as well as hers." He ran his long fingers through dark hair then smoothed it self-consciously.

"I'm back in the Patrol after being out of it for a few years and I'm back for one purpose. To try to stop some of the illegal operations that criminals are using our borders for. The Mexico-U.S. border is especially vulnerable because of its isolation and few inhabitants. To say that it's dangerous is a statement that could apply to the streets of Dahlonega or any other city in the United States. But when I say dangerous as it applies to Region Seven of our Regional Command, picture it in ten foot high red letters."

Beth sat stiffly, her fists clenched beside her, eyes darkening with anger as he spoke, but she didn't interrupt. It would do no good; Brand Page was going to have his say whether she approved or not.

"The people we are hunting are not amateurs. They are killers, thieves, dealers in human flesh in ways you would never be able to imagine. They are not above selling our country or any foreign country down the river for a few dollars and whoever gets in their way will be disposed of without a thought."

No one spoke, and Brand reached into his pocket to bring out a folded paper Beth recognized as the letter she had opened by mistake. He looked at it a moment before he handed it to Jim.

"I want you to read this before you agree to let Beth go to Nogales."

Jim took the letter, gray eyes so like Beth's studying the man in front of him. He looked from Beth to Mary Ann before he unfolded the letter.

"Read it aloud," Brand said.

Jim cleared his throat and read: "'Dear Brand: Before I congratulate you on your outstanding performance at the Academy (and, I might add, always), I want you to know that I'm sticking with my decision to assign Beth Page as your partner in the problem we discussed. She has shown marked potential as an excellent officer and her grades are as good as yours. You know as well as I do that we have few females who can perform that way. In addition to keeping you on an even keel with these dangerous criminals you'll most certainly meet, it will also get the Equal Employment Opportunity Office off our backs about hiring women.'''

Jim looked up, eyes narrowed, his lips tightly drawn. "I don't care if he is your superior, that's a weak reason to put anyone inexperienced in a dangerous position."

"I don't make the rules and sometimes don't play by them, sir. That's why I'm telling you this much. If you can talk Beth out of going, I'll put her somewhere she's relatively safe. Where this assignment will take us is not."

"No," Beth said, standing to walk close to him, looking defiantly into his stern face. "My orders say Region Seven and that's where I'm going. If you don't want me, you get rid of me. You're putting Dad in a bad position and it's not his decision. It's mine."

The silence grew as he glared at her and she returned his gaze without flinching. "Beth, look, if anything happens to you, I'm the one who must tell Jim and Mary Ann."

"And who do I tell if something happens to you, Brand?"

It was a long, tension-charged moment before he said quietly, "Just report it to headquarters, Beth."

He took the letter from Jim's unresisting fingers and folded it to replace it in his pocket. "I wanted you to know what she's letting herself in for."

Mary Ann spoke for the first time. "Do you know about Jud Chambers, Brand?"

"Yes. I've read the case several times."

"He was very dear to all of us and we understand Beth's feelings." She smiled at the girl standing stiff and straight in front of Brand. "We'll go along with Beth's decision."

A flicker of something like anguish flashed in his dark gray eyes as Brand continued to look at Beth, and he swallowed hard before he straightened, nodding to Jim and Mary Ann.

"My boss knows I'm always careful, but he's depending on my being more so if Beth is there. And I will be." He gave Beth a tight smile. "It may not be enough."

Jim got up and poured two drinks, passing one to Brand. The conversation lapsed as they sat, each with his own thoughts. Beth was the first to move.

"I'll say good night." She kissed her mother and as she passed Jim, she nodded. "You're all right even if you are my dad."

"Wait, Beth, I'll walk up with you."

Surprised, Beth turned as Brand gave her parents a brief smile and followed her. He took her hand as they walked upstairs and, at her door, drew her into his arms. He smiled only a little as he bent to kiss her, his mouth moving lightly on hers. He caressed her lips with the tip of his tongue, stirring response deep inside her. Eyes closed, she remained still, her hands resting on his ribs.

He lifted his head and her lashes swung upward. "Good night, Beth," he said and moved down the hall.

She watched until he entered the far bedroom and the door closed behind him.

As she stood leaning against the doorjamb she felt warmed by Brand's kiss, but memories of their argument suddenly invaded her mind, recalling her anger. The conflicting emotions vied all through the night.

Chapter Five

"If what Brand says is true, Beth, it wouldn't make you look bad to ask for a transfer to another branch of Customs. No one would blame you," Jim told her as they sat at the kitchen table after Brand left early the next morning.

"We discussed this when I went in, Dad, remember? Conditions haven't changed. Brand explains them in graphic terms that make you sit up and take notice. Chances are that I'll never encounter those problems." Her glance went to her mother's face and her voice softened. "You'll worry about me, of course, but you would if I taught school in Atlanta."

"You must admit this is different, Beth," Mary Ann said.

"Yes."

They were silent, each with his own thoughts. Danger was there. How much danger, neither could guess, nor did they want to. In the line of duty of all law enforcement agencies, danger was an element not to be ignored. You could only depend on your training—and a lot of luck.

"I want to stay in. Perhaps after this tour of duty is up, I'll want to get out, but not yet."

Her dad nodded, and after a while he stood up. "If you want the little car, honey, we'd better get all the papers together so we can transfer the title to you. "What's your reporting date?"

"September twenty-first."

IT WAS JUST LIKE HER PARENTS to give their understanding and support and, during the long Labor Day weekend, they talked and planned as though she were going on a job as normal as teaching. They eased their worries into the background and enjoyed being together, taking a canoe out on Dockery Lake to fish, catching nothing but a small bream which they threw back.

She joined them at a dance, wearing the navy-blue dress she had bought the year before but hadn't worn because of Jud's death.

As she sat watching the dancers, she recalled each step and word she and Brand had shared—was it only two days before?

One night, Jim brought out the Scrabble game and they argued over words until the phone rang. She was laughing at Jim's insistence that *ario* was a word when she picked up the receiver.

"It's something to do with music," he argued.

"Maybe you mean *arioso*, dad, but you don't have room for that," she told him, speaking into the phone. "Hello?"

"Beth?" It was Brand and she wondered at the weakness that suddenly replaced the strength in her slim legs.

Breathless for the moment, she swallowed and said, "Hello, Brand. Where are you?"

The deep laughter sent a wave of delicious question marks skidding along the edge of her brief shorts where she could almost feel his touch again, as he had touched her on Saturday morning.

"I'm at home."

"Already? I thought it took three days or more." She looked up to find Jim and Mary Ann watching her and mouthed his name to them although they had heard her question.

"I didn't stop Saturday night except for a couple of hours at a rest stop. How was the weekend?"

Beth went over the unprofitable fishing trip and the dance. "We're getting the car papers ready to transfer the ownership to me so I'll have transportation to Arizona."

His voice lowered perceptibly as he asked, "You didn't change your mind?"

"No. And I won't. You'll have to work for that all alone, Brand."

There was a moment of silence and she heard his indrawn breath. "I just wanted to thank your parents again for having me and to let you know the trailer will be ready for you when you arrive. The twenty-first, isn't it?"

"Yes."

"You're going to call me before you leave there?"

"Yes, Brand, I will."

"Okay, Beth. See you soon."

She hung up the phone and walked slowly back to

the table where her parents waited for her to resume the game.

"He's already at home?" Jim asked. "He was really traveling."

"He drove most of Saturday night. I won't be able to do that. I'd go to sleep and miss my exit." Beth laughed, holding the thought of Brand's call close to her. He didn't really expect her to change her mind so why did he call? *Common courtesy, of course, Beth,* she reasoned, and picked the work *mussel* to win the Scrabble game.

SHE VISITED OLD FRIENDS, ran track at the high school where she had graduated eons before, felt a thrill of ownership as she signed the papers making the compact car hers. It was two years old with eleven thousand miles on it and, knowing Jim, in perfect running condition. On Friday, she drove up to Helen, walking the streets of the picturesque little town still alive with holiday celebrations. It was suppertime when she pulled into the driveway at the front of the house.

Jim and Mary Ann were waiting for her, ready to go out to eat, and she hugged them both. "Love the car, Dad. Last chance to change your mind about keeping it—but don't you dare."

He shook his head. "We ordered the van and it should be here within six weeks, in time for a trip to Baldy Mountain before the snows come."

They ate at the stately old Carriage House and were home by eight o'clock. Beth was pleasantly tired and lay in the middle of the living-room floor as they carried on idle conversation. The phone rang and Jim stretched to reach the instrument.

As he listened to the other party talking, his eyes settled on Beth, who had rolled over on her stomach.

"How are things in the wild west, Brand?"

At the question, Beth opened her eyes wide and listened. A moment later, he said, "Yes, she's here," and handed the receiver to Beth. As she sat up, gray eyes questioning him, he and Mary Ann got up to leave the room.

"Don't tell me Arizona did secede just because of me?" she asked, conscious of a slight tremor in her voice.

His soft laugh came across thousands of miles. "Afraid not, Beth. There's been a slight alteration of plans, however. I want you to meet me in El Paso on the seventeenth. There's an interagency briefing at the intelligence center there and you need to attend. We can arrange for you to take the balance of your leave later."

Well, nothing like getting into the thick of it even before reporting time, was her surprised thought.

"If I leave here on Tuesday, will that give me enough time?"

"The first meeting is early Friday morning so you'll have plenty of time. I've made reservations for us at the La Quinta on the interstate near the Drug Enforcement Administration. Almost within walking distance if you're energetic."

"All right, Brand. I'll be there."

"Did you get your car?"

She laughed. "Oh, yes, and is it a dream? The one I

sold when I went into the Patrol was ten years old and about on its last mile. Thank goodness for improvements since then.''

"I'm flying to El Paso and will drive back with you if that's okay?''

"Of course, Brand. According to my figures, it's only about a six hour drive from El Paso to Nogales.''

"Only?''

"Well, compared to three or four days, it sounds like a short time.''

"You'll be tired enough by then that six hours will seem more than that, probably,'' he reminded her gently. "I'll see you Thursday, Beth.''

A briefing; her first as a Patrol officer graduated from the Federal Law Enforcement Training Center. In classes briefings had been simulated and actions taken on information gained from those briefings worked out by the students. Remembering the day she froze with the gun in her hand, she shivered. It had never happened since that day, but what if it had been real? No second chances except in training.

Look, Beth, you forget the doubts and look at the positive side, she cautioned herself.

And in the days that followed her conversation with Brand, she did just that. For Jud. For Beth. For everyone affected by the criminal element she would be fighting. She would do her best.

IT WASN'T EASY leaving Jim and Mary Ann; she hadn't expected it to be. Although tears were beneath the surface, none fell.

At five o'clock that Tuesday morning, she pulled from the familiar driveway, turning the car lights on to shine through the foggy mist that lay close to the fragrant earth. She was well past Atlanta, with the cruise control set to rest her legs, when she turned off the lights.

Her thirteen-hour drive behind her, Beth slept quickly and was up and on her way again by five the next morning, stopping for breakfast after driving two hours. The hours and miles swept by as she watched the scenery change from heavy greenness to rolling hills to high desert as she entered the last phase of her trip.

Interstate 10 intersected with Interstate 20 which she had followed all the way from Atlanta and took a straight westerly direction. It was two in the afternoon as she entered the city limits of El Paso, to her untrained eye still out in the middle of nowhere. She topped a rise to see the city lying in front of her.

A few miles on she saw the sign for the La Quinta Inn. Odd name she thought. The literal English translation of the Spanish name meant "fifth one down." *Fifth one down from what?* she wondered, as she parked near the office.

Inside, she inquired about her room.

"Page?" the young lady repeated, looking at her cards. She frowned. "I'm sorry, ma'am, we don't have a reservation in that name."

Beth hesitated. Brand would never make a mistake like that; he was too thorough in his instructions.

"There should be two—" she began.

The woman smiled at her. "Perhaps your reservation

is at the other motel, ma'am. There are two La Quintas. Let me call."

Beth had meant to say two "Pages" but the woman had taken it to mean two motels and that had rung a bell for her.

Beth breathed easier and waited, seeing by the expression on the girl's face that the second place did have the reservation.

"That's it," the receptionist said, relaxing as she faced Beth. "Going west on the interstate, the motel is about three miles from here on the left side of the highway. Take the Trowbridge Street exit, turn left under the overpass, and it's right there."

"Thank you," she said and went back to climb into her car. She'd be glad to stretch out for a couple of hours to get the stiff kinks out of her body.

Finding the motel without trouble, Beth walked into the office to find the young man already had her card out ready for her to sign in.

"Mr. Page is already here, ma'am," he said. She looked at the card. It was a double room signed for Beth and Brand Page.

"We aren't together," she told him.

A puzzled look came into his face. "Not together? But I thought—"

"No. I need a single room. I'm not related to Mr. Page."

It took a bit more explaining but finally, she was given a key to a single room and, once inside, breathed a sigh of relief. Brand was already here so that was good and she wondered if he had thought about a possible mix-up of the names.

Probably never crossed his mind, she thought. She stretched on the bed wondering if he was already checking out their status with DEA.

His room was at the end of the hall from her, but she didn't want to disturb him; he could be resting also. She was asleep in moments.

Her sleep was interrupted by the knock on the door and her thoughts sluggishly refused to come together enough to realize where she was.

The second knock was followed immediately by Brand's voice. "Beth?"

"Oh," she said, sitting up quickly. Brushing at the heavy wave of hair swinging against her cheek, she moved to the door and opened it.

Brand smiled, taking in the shirt pulled partly from her jeans and the crease, caused by a wrinkle in the spread, across one cheek.

Returning the smile, she stepped aside as he came into the room and leaned against the door.

"No trouble?" he asked, his eyes going from the tousled silver-blond hair to her bare feet.

She laughed, pushing at her hair. "Not on the trip." She explained about the two motels with the same name and about the double room assigned to them.

An odd expression touched his face. "I didn't even notice when I signed the register. Why didn't you leave it that way and save the government some money?"

"The government?" she asked, trying to ignore the look on his face. Perhaps he had thought about a mix-up.

"Sure. They have to reimburse us since this is classified as temporary duty from a permanent station."

She motioned him to the chair by the windows and sat on the edge of the bed. "Do you already know what the briefings are about?"

He nodded. "They have plans for us on a stakeout starting Sunday night, a day ahead of your reporting date. That's why I had you meet me here. There's no leeway in the time."

"What type of stakeout?"

"Surveillance. Informants from across the border got word that traffic has started in another commodity as yet unidentified. Officials have come down so hard and fast on their drug rings that they are curtailing those activities in favor of something else. That's all the details we have: just that it's a new twist." He studied her face as he went on. "It won't be pretty, whatever it is."

"Will we know by the time we leave here?"

"Right now it's all speculation on the part of the Drug Enforcement Administration and the El Paso Intelligence Center. Not only do they not know exactly what we'll be facing, but the only help we can expect is from two officers stationed at Lukeville."

She thought over what he was saying, picturing some of the stakeout procedures they had used during training. They had been rough and primitive; what they faced would be even more so, she was certain. A new twist, something cold and deadly. Brand's voice told her that without her having to ask.

"Why don't we go out to Cattleman's Steakhouse for dinner tonight if you aren't too tired?" he asked. "It's twenty-five miles out in the desert but well worth the trip."

"Sounds good," she decided immediately. "I'm starved."

He glanced at his watch. "I'll pick you up in an hour. That'll put us out there about the time we can watch the sunset. It's spectacular."

"You've been there before?"

"Yes. It's been a couple of years, but I'm sure neither the food nor the sunsets have changed." He started to the door. "Jeans are the uniform of the day." He smiled. "I'll be back."

The door clicked shut behind him and she heard him turn the knob to check to see if it locked then his footsteps faded down the hall. She opened her suitcase to pull out fresh jeans and a soft blue T-shirt with an appliquéd "B" over her left breast.

A quick shower revived her and she brushed her heavy hair back to fasten it with combs, letting the hair around her face form small curls in front of her ears. The tiredness showed in her face and she added a small amount of color to her cheeks. When the knock sounded, she was ready.

Brand drove her car, heading east in the direction from which she had come. When he turned from the interstate onto a two-lane road heading north, he said, "It's really a dude ranch called Indian Cliffs. They have hay rides and cater to big parties but their steaks are what puts them on the map."

Beth's eyes were on the road in front of them where two small cottontail rabbits played, suddenly skittering off the side of the road. A tiny desert squirrel sat up on his hind legs and took off as the car got close to him.

"That's about all you see in the desert, rabbits and

desert squirrels. Unless you're unlucky enough to come upon some of the snakes that claim it as home.''

"Is this like the desert around Nogales?" she asked.

He nodded. "This is more civilized."

Looking around, she turned back to him. "How?"

He grinned but his eyes were suddenly serious. "We have mostly snakes, the two-legged being the more dangerous of the species."

She was quiet until he pointed ahead of them. Crossing the road at a leisurely pace was a long-legged, long-bodied bird. "A roadrunner." Before she could comment, he said, "And there's the restaurant."

On a high dune sat a low building made of sandstone, arches and flat roof typical of the southwestern style of architecture. They turned onto a narrow dirt lane that wound between horse stables and a shallow salt lake, inclining sharply to bring them into the parking lot in the back of the restaurant. A cowboy on a sleek gelding directed them to a parking place.

As Brand opened the car door for her, he took her arm and turned her to look toward the west. A bank of dark gray clouds partly hid the sun, turning the diffused gold rays into oranges and reds.

"It'll be about right for us to really get a good look from the terrace behind the bar."

The aromas coming from the kitchen were mouthwatering to say the least and Beth remembered that she hadn't eaten since her late breakfast around eleven o'clock. She touched her stomach.

"Boy, I can't wait."

Brand laughed. "Yes, you can. It may be a little while before we get a table."

"You're kidding," she moaned.

"It's a popular place," he said looking down at her. "But maybe they'll take pity on you."

Inside they found they would have about ten minutes to wait and he led her through the rustic hallway toward the terrace he had mentioned, stopping first at the bar.

Drinks in hand, they wandered out onto the porch where several others were gathered to watch the sunset. A balustrade offered a sitting place and they sat sideways, looking out over the flatness marred only by lumpy sand dunes and high mesas scattered about.

She tasted her margarita, licking her lips to remove the salt that had crystallized on the cold glass. The sharp fresh taste was pleasant to her dry throat.

They watched the colors deepen, change and brighten as the clouds shifted as though changing color slides for their benefit. It was a fantastic display.

A few minutes later, Brand's name was called and they followed the hostess to a table by the window. Their view still encompassed the setting sun and overlooked the area where a big hay wagon stood after passengers debarked.

When their meal was placed in front of them, Brand cut her a piece of the steak that was already causing her mouth to water. Halfway through the meal, she raised her head to look at him.

"You're right. It's the best tasting steak I've ever had."

"You deserve it after all the cafeteria meals at Glynco," he said.

She stiffened, waiting, but he didn't pursue the subject further. He made small talk by mentioning other places of interest around the city.

"Too bad we won't have time to go across to Juarez while you're here, but you can do some shopping for Mary Ann across in Nogales, Mexico."

They left the restaurant and headed back toward El Paso, driving west straight toward the craggy outline of the Franklin Mountains. By the time they reached the motel, she was half asleep.

"How long will we be here?" she asked as he unlocked her door and handed the key back to her.

"We'll leave here Saturday morning. I imagine our orders will give us a specific time to be on the stakeout."

"Do you already know where it will be?"

He nodded. "I'll pick you up in time for breakfast tomorrow; we'll have a break during the day, but I'm not sure how long we get for lunch so we'd better get a good meal to start out." He bent to kiss her cheek.

"Good night, Beth."

She thought briefly about what was in store for her tomorrow—her first official duty. Everything she'd been taught in Glynco was quickly run back through her mind. Her training had prepared her for anything, hadn't it?

BETH HAD NEVER KNOWN briefings or any type of orientation to start on time, but this one did. Looking around at the others in the small windowless room, she frowned. It certainly was a small group and she was the only female. A small thrill of apprehension caused her to swallow over a dry throat.

Brand's attention was centered on two men who stood by the podium at the front of the room. One was tall, a little stoop shouldered, with thinning white hair. The other was about the same age, balding, with piercing black eyes that scoured the room, settling on Beth.

As her eyes met the black ones from the front of the room she stiffened. Another one that didn't want women in his domain. She felt Brand turn to look at her and she blinked before meeting his gaze. He pointed to the name at the top of the single sheet of paper he held.

Geoffrey Montague. She frowned, trying to remember where she had seen the name. With a shock, she remembered. He was a four-star general assigned to the Energy Department's Safeguards and Security Division Command Center.

A question formed on her lips at the same time that General Montague said, "Good morning, lady and gentlemen." It was a pointed use of the single noun, but Beth sat looking straight at him and didn't even flinch at being singled out. It didn't matter to her.

He got straight to the point. "This briefing is going to be just that—brief. Most of you here are backup for the action that we expect could happen. Let me emphasize that—*could* happen. We have no information that guarantees we'll see any of what is about to be shown here."

A slide projector was turned on and the light focused on a screen behind the general. "Brand Page will be in charge of the surveillance and stakeout. Beth Page will be with him in the danger area. Ward Sutherland and Milt Spivey will be between Benson and the intersection of Highway 90. The danger area has been identified as the Madera Canyon just back of Mount Wright-son."

He paused to let that sink in. Beth was conscious of Brand's fingers closing around her hand and she drew in her breath as General Montague went on.

"The operation is secret; no one outside this room knows about it. After you have seen the film, we will take a break. This is the only time the film will be shown; remember what you see."

The title filled the screen in dark red letters: "Riding with Suicide Jockeys." Depicted was a convoy of common carrier trucks strung out on a highway, driving at exactly fifty-five miles per hour as shown when the camera zeroed in on a speedometer. In the front seat were three men dressed as any ordinary truck driver would be, in jeans and dungaree jacket.

There the likeness to ordinary truck drivers ended. The man on the passenger side held an automatic weapon between his knees and his eyes went the perimeter from directly right of the truck to the left corner of the windshield. The second man was in the short seat back of the driver; he held a submachine gun. His gaze went from the left corner of the windshield to his left all the way to the road behind them. The driver watched the front of the road and the back through the rearview mirror.

The camera angled to the back of the truck, showing the interior. Beth suddenly could hear her heartbeat and her throat went dry. The truck was loaded with nuclear weapons!

She blinked as the lights came on and she looked around her. Each face must have mirrored what she was feeling: dazed disbelief. She was careful not to look at Brand but put the hand he had been holding against her thigh. It was warm; the other hand was icy.

"This afternoon, specific orders and instructions will be given. I'll see you back here at one sharp," General Montague said and marched out the door without a backward look.

Outside the briefing room, Brand touched her arm as two men came up to him.

"Beth, meet Milt Spivey and Ward Sutherland, the two mentioned that will be in Benson. They're from our Lukeville area." He had named them as the only other two officers besides them who patrolled near Nogales when he tried to dissuade her from the job.

Ward grinned, showing white teeth beneath a thick sandy mustache. His big hand swallowed hers and was in no hurry to let go as he looked her over, blue-green eyes showing an immediate interest in Brand's newly acquired partner.

Withdrawing her hand, she held it out to Milt who gave her a shy grin. Thick rusty hair fought against any attempt at control, a thick tuft sticking up above the smooth crown at the back, his face almost a solid freckle.

"I didn't think the old man would give us a lunch break," Ward said. "He usually goes straight through when he's down here. Can't stand to be away from that job of his more than a few hours."

"He's worried," Brand told him. "And from what we saw on that film, he has reason to be."

Beth said nothing, knowing she wouldn't be told the complete story until they returned to the secure briefing room. She followed them outside and they all climbed into her car with Brand driving. He seemed to know his way around the city and in a few minutes they had stopped outside a stucco building with a sign that said Forti's Mexican Elder.

"Like Mexican food?" Brand asked.

"Not the kind you get in Georgia," she said.

He grinned. "This is definitely different."

As they were served the three men discussed general topics relating to the Patrol, but nothing was mentioned about the film they had seen. Uneasiness filled Beth as she thought about the convoy of nuclear weapons. Such a secret mission couldn't be discussed outside a secure room.

"Ever been to Arizona, Beth?" Ward asked as she bit into a tostado she dipped into the green sauce.

Gasping at her first real taste of chili sauce, she sipped ice water before she shook her head: "I have been warned, however," she managed after a few seconds, her eyes watering.

He nodded. "Listen to Brand. He knows the country."

As they went on talking Beth concentrated on eating. *Listen to Brand? How can I help but listen to him? He's my supervisor—or haven't you heard?*

Whatever it was she had ordered was really good even if it did take the skin off her tongue.

When they returned to the briefing room and were waiting for the others, she asked Brand, "Is this all the people who will be involved in the operation?"

He nodded. "The fewer people we have on this job, the better off we'll be. It's guesswork at best, and if we do find what General Montague says we might, a few well-trained people work better than a crowd at a time like this.''

When General Montague appeared everyone filed in and grew quiet as he prepared to brief them.

''Our informants on this job are ones that have been dependable in the past; therefore we cannot afford to ignore their warnings. I gave some thought to postponing this particular shipment, but to do so will place too many people in danger unnecessarily.'' He paused to look over the small audience.

''Contact among all participants in the surveillance will be at a minimum. If a hijacking of the weapons is planned you can rest assured that it is of greatest importance to the people who are after the cargo. They will be prepared to go all the way to carry out their plans. We must do the same.'' His voice was quiet and somehow therefore all the more deadly.

Beth shivered and felt Brand turn to look at her, but she stared at General Montague as he turned to leave the stage.

''That's all,'' the man with the black eyes Brand had identified as Lewis Saven, top security man for the Energy Department, told them. ''Brand Page will meet with his group at sixteen hundred hours Saturday in his office in Nogales.''

Brand spoke to several of the men as they left, then looked at her. ''We could make it to Nogales tonight, if you like.''

''That's fine with me.''

''We're spending the night with Milt's uncle here,'' Ward said, ''and we'll be there tomorrow afternoon.''

An hour later, Brand and Beth were heading west on Interstate 10, driving straight through El Paso toward Las Cruces. The Franklin Mountain chain gave way to the Sacramento range on the right and outside of Las Cruces they ran into the awesome splendor of the Organ Mountains.

"Have you ever been involved in this type of stakeout before?" Beth asked, unable to conceal her curiosity any longer.

"No. This is a new type of action from terrorist groups infiltrating into the States from Central America." His voice was calm, showing no anxiety at all.

Beth glanced at him, but he was watching the road, and she settled back in the seat, thinking about the briefing. Tomorrow she would find out exactly what was expected of her.

"They really do look like pipe organs, don't they?" she remarked, gazing at the rugged ridge of rocks.

"I don't know what a pipe organ looks like," he said, smiling at the expression in her wide gray eyes. "But I have to admit, they are plenty rough looking. I wouldn't have liked crossing them in a covered wagon."

When he stopped the car in front of a truck stop, she looked around at the sign that said "Benson."

"This is where Milt and Ward will be hanging out Sunday?" she asked when he made no move to leave the car.

"Between here and the highway where you and I will be."

She was silent for a long time picturing the scenes that had been shown in the briefing room at DEA. Of all the things they had covered in their field training, they had only touched briefly on dealings with terrorists and it had seemed far-out to even consider being involved with such an outfit. Brand had mentioned the FALN and that it was moving along the Gulf Coast, but no one had dreamed another more deadly group would precede them.

If the terrorists succeeded in commandeering the convoy of nuclear weapons, what then? That convoy traveled under top secret conditions—but someone knew about the movement of the valuable—and dangerous—cargo. How?

"Afraid?" Brand asked softly.

Raising her head to meet his dark gray gaze, she nodded slowly. "Are you?"

His expression changed as he took in the almost heart-shaped face with wide, light-colored eyes, the silver blond of her hair, the small white teeth biting into one corner of her lower lip.

He looked at the building in front of them. "Yes," he said. "I'd rather we were afraid than foolhardy. The people we will be dealing with are determined, deadly, and greedy. It's an explosive combination. As long as we remember that and continue to outthink them, we can win."

"But why so few people to try and stop them, Brand? What chance will we have to protect the convoy if they do attack?"

"Informants say the group planning the heist is very small. This is because it draws less attention. It also means that the members are deadly serious and will let nothing stand in the way of getting this shipment if they can possibly help it."

After a moment to let that sink in, he went on.

"We aren't entirely alone, however. Backups are all along the mountain ridges down to the Mexican border with four special agents at Sonoita. They'll be in touch with all the others involved. We can't have radio contact because of the possibility of detection. Ward and Milt will be the roving patrol to keep us informed about any progress made by the convoy or any attempt at hijacking. You and I will be in the direct route they'll take should they get the weapons."

He turned to smile at her. "Let's get a sandwich while we're here."

They had a sandwich and iced tea inside the small but crowded café and as they came outside, Beth asked, "Would you like me to drive?"

"No, it isn't that far now."

She was glad to let him drive and she put her head back against the seat, closing her eyes. It was dark and there wasn't much she could see anyway. When Brand turned from the interstate, she sat up.

He gave her a smiling glance. "Just about eighteen miles now," he said, and a little later, "That's the way to Patagonia." He pointed to his left.

She strained to see the mesquite-dotted landscape, but there wasn't much visible other than the outline of the ragged mountain peaks on both sides of them.

"This is where we turn right, Beth, when we go on our infamous criminal hunts."

A long, slim forefinger pointed to the west and she remembered his comment: *You turn right at Nogales, straight to hell.* It was just as well she couldn't see what lay out there.

Chapter Six

Beth was awake early on Saturday morning, her body stiff and sore from the several days of riding. The layover in El Paso helped a little but not much. She needed a track to run and wondered if one would be nearby.

All her clothing unpacked and hung in the compact storage areas of the trailer, she looked around at her new home. It was neat and clean and private. Better than she expected, but according to Brand she wouldn't spend a lot of time in it. They had lots of plans for the two-person patrol that they now were.

Opening her front door, she saw a truck pull into the yard of the first trailer Brand had pointed out as their office. Trailer number six was his, located a few yards in front of hers which was number ten.

Odd numbers, she thought, and watched a man in a Customs Patrol uniform enter the first trailer. Brand said his administrative officer was Alfredo Ruiz. She started up the gravel drive past the number six trailer when Brand came out.

He waited till she got even with him and asked, "Did you lock your door?"

"No, I'm only—"

"Lock it every time you leave to walk to the back of the trailer, Beth. That's an order." Something in his voice made her stop and stare at him, then look back at her innocent looking living quarters.

"I mean it. Every time. Your car too."

They walked on in silence and he held the door for her to walk through in front of him. They hadn't even exchanged greetings.

"Brand," the dark-eyed man exclaimed. "I wasn't expecting you till later today."

They shook hands and Brand said, "We decided to come in last night. Beth, this is Alfredo, best administrator in the Patrol. He keeps us up-to-date on regulations, sees that we have orders when we travel, and makes sure someone remembers us on payday."

"Alfredo," she said and smiled up at him. Liquid dark eyes surveyed the slim figure in front of him and he grinned, showing white teeth behind a black bush of mustache.

"You're right, Brand, she doesn't look like any Customs Officer I've ever seen before."

Beth stiffened. "I wasn't aware I was supposed to fit into a stereotype."

Brand grinned at her indignant expression. "You must admit there aren't many around that look like you, Beth."

"Get used to seeing me because I'll be here a while," she told him and watched his eyes darken and

the straight line form around his mouth. For a breathless moment, she felt his kiss again, and as her eyes
held his she could see that he too remembered. It gave
her a strange feeling of satisfaction to know that he was
forced to remember what he probably would rather not.

"Speaking of payday, do you need to draw an advance?" he asked.

"Advance?"

"Payday was yesterday and it's hard to tell where
your pay card is. Will you need money before next payday?"

"No, thank you."

Alfredo had made coffee and now handed each of
them a cup and they sat in the small metal chairs near
the front of the trailer office.

"We'll have a meeting at sixteen hundred hours this
afternoon, Alfredo. Milt and Ward will be here. Did we
get what the OPLANS Region was supposed to send
with the new appendix?"

"Yes. Only one copy. It's secret."

Brand nodded. "That's okay."

They finished the coffee and Brand showed her the
combination to the one safe she'd use and all the forms
they would have to fill out. "When you finish with a
classified plan, just give it to Alfredo. It's easier to have
one person taking care of them, then we know who to
blame if we can't find them." He smiled at her, and as
he continued to look at her she turned away.

"You'll have to wear a cap on that hair, Beth. Out in
the desert at night with the moon shining, it'll be like a
spotlight."

She nodded. "I have a fatigue cap that covers it when I put my hair up on top of my head."

They went through other plans and he filled her in on who their contacts were at the headquarters in downtown Nogales.

"We don't bother them unless we have to and they conveniently forget us when possible. We get along that way."

At three thirty Ward and Milt arrived and they went into the back room of the office to get specific orders for the stakeout they would start at midnight.

"Beth and I will be in Madera Canyon. Milt, you and Ward will patrol blacked out from the interstate toward us every two hours."

"Why would they come through the canyon, Brand? Seems to me Sonoita would be a more likely spot, especially if they plan to stop the trucks near Benson."

"Four agents are on the outskirts of Sonoita. They have the special flares if they see anything suspicious."

"Suppose the informant was lying?" Beth asked.

"He's paid good money not to lie," Ward told her.

"Perhaps with what's at stake, someone across the way might pay them more."

"Or kill them if they don't give them the information they want," Brand said, adding quietly, "It's a chance we always take."

No one said anything and he said, "Okay, everyone at their starting points at midnight. If the trucks are on time, we should know something by four in the morning."

Beth left them and returned to her trailer. She had

until ten o'clock to think over the plot and the plan they were to put into operation.

The trucks they were looking for were in a convoy of thirty. Designed to look like any other long-distance haulers, they carried nuclear weapons and the eye-catching title of the movie "Suicide Jockeys"—the name given to the people who drove the trucks. Informants told them an element of a terrorist group from South America had planned to confiscate at least half of the convoy for the weapons. Where and how they planned to do this was the unknown portion of the plan. The information had been on short notice and few officers were available for use in a stakeout that was doubtful to say the least. Not many criminals, no matter how desperate for money or weapons, would put a plan such as had been broached into effect, but they couldn't afford to ignore the warning. General Montague would never allow the U.S. government to ignore the warning. A small force was sometimes better operationally too, in such cases, Brand told her.

At any rate, there were eight of them with conventional weapons against a group that might acquire other than conventional weapons. Somewhat unfair odds. According to Brand, this was the usual way Customs Patrol worked—understaffed.

She should call home, Beth thought, and since this would be her last chance, she went back outside, remembering to lock her door. She stuck her head in the door of the office.

"I saw a telephone booth up the street. I'm going to call home."

"No, Beth," Brand said, coming from the back room.

"Use this telephone here and bill it to my number."

"But—"

"The first thing you were taught at the Academy was to take orders. Now do what you're told."

The hardness of his voice made her stare, and Alfredo stopped what he was doing to glance at them. Slowly Beth walked into the office, anger doing a slow burn through her body. Being a supervisor didn't entail ordering her personal life around, she was sure, but she didn't want to argue in front of Alfredo.

Brand picked up the phone, gave her home number in Dahlonega without asking her, listened, then handed her the receiver.

The ring was cut off in the middle and Jim said, "Hello?"

Swallowing over the confused anger in her throat, she looked away from Brand as she said, "Dad, it's Beth."

"Beth, honey, where are you?"

Smiling at his automatic question, she talked quietly to him then to Mary Ann, promising to write soon. Hanging up the phone, she turned to the door, murmuring her thanks over the sudden lump in her throat, not sure if she was aggravated with Brand or homesick after talking to her parents.

She was old enough not to sulk when told what to do by her superiors, she thought, and not to be homesick when she left home to go to the wild desert twenty-five hundred miles away.

"Try to rest. I'll call you in plenty of time," Brand said behind her.

She nodded and left the trailer, standing outside of

hers to look around at the wildness. Brand had not exaggerated. For miles there was desert splotched with mesquite, salt cedar, and tumble weeds, spreading to the base of mountains that turned blue and brown in the late afternoon sun. Breathing in the unaccustomed dry air, she realized her nose had opened up completely and her breath went deep into her chest. She grinned. At home this time of year, she was forever trying to get her air passages open.

At least one benefit from this barren wasteland. It must not be all bad.

Inside the trailer she stood a moment, reached back to lock the door, and went to look for stationery. Smitty would want to know what was going on with them— that is, if she came down out of her clouds long enough, she and Ted.

There was a knock at her door and the knob turned, but she had listened to Brand's warning. She waited.

"Beth?" The name was spoken with a little uncertainty and she knew a fierce satisfaction that he hadn't been able to find something else to reprimand her for.

"Yes?" She didn't move toward the door.

"I want to talk to you, Beth."

Why? she wondered. *That's all we've done all day and you still haven't said anything.*

She opened the door and stood aside as Brand entered, stooping automatically. As he turned to look down at her she motioned to the one big chair in the room and went to sit on one of the stools in front of the breakfast bar separating the living room from the kitchen area.

"Do you have any boots?" he asked.

"Shoe boots, not high ones."

He nodded. "They'll do. First time in Nogales, go to Cork's and get some plain black boots. They protect your legs when you're crawling around in the desert."

His eyes went over the faded jeans and Pink Panther T-shirt and a half smile touched his mouth. "Wear a darker shirt, preferably long sleeves. Other than that, what you're wearing is the type of uniform you need out here."

"We don't wear fatigues?"

"Not this time. Take a jacket. It gets chilly in that canyon."

He continued to look at her and his eyes changed from warm to a sudden distant expression as his gaze came back to rest on her mouth for an instant.

"Your baptism under fire will be tonight, Beth. If we're lucky, our informants were wrong and the strike will be somewhere else rather than here."

"If it isn't somewhere else, Brand? Are you uneasy because you're stuck with me or because you have an idea it's going to get messy?"

He stood up and walked toward her. He reached to lift her from the stool, pulling her to him. She stiffened, trying to pull away, but he held her, bending until his mouth rested on hers, gently forcing her lips apart.

For a moment she resisted, then relaxed against him, her arms going around him to hold him close. Her heart speeded up as he went over her mouth with his, the tip of his tongue touching the corner. His hands left her body to frame her face, holding it immovable as the pressure on her lips increased. Her arms around him tightened in response, her body moved closer to him of its own accord, as lightning struck the nerve ends in every part of her.

She was suddenly free as he pushed her away and turned toward the door. Her breath was audible in the room, but he didn't look at her as he started out.

"I trust my partner because it's necessary, Beth. I also worry. I'll call you before ten."

She stood there looking at the door. The kiss felt like good-bye. Her skin was clammy with the feeling of emptiness she had when she thought of Jud. She stood for a long time staring at the closed door before going to lie on the bed at the back of the trailer. It was cool and pleasant and she listened to the hum of the big metal box on top of the trailer that Brand explained held the air coolers used in the dry desert.

It was a long time before the sound drowned out her thoughts and lulled her to sleep.

THE VEHICLE BRAND DROVE toward their stakeout location was an unmarked Customs truck. Beneath the seat were their packs including the .357 Magnum most Patrol officers preferred.

A sliver of moon and a million stars gave a ghostly appearance to the rugged terrain and when the truck stopped and lights were out, they seemed to be alone in the world.

"Stay in the truck until I give you the signal, Beth. I'll be a hundred yards away in that arroyo." He pointed in front of the truck. She nodded.

Rolling down the window so she could hear the shrill call of the night bird as their signal, she leaned against the cool vinyl upholstery and waited. A light breeze came in, stirring her hair, and she reached in her pocket to pull out the olive drab fatigue cap. Twisting her hair into a heavy roll, she pushed it up on top of her head, anchoring it with a comb, and placed the baseball-type cap on it. It would perhaps save her from a reprimand.

A sound from in front of her brought her gaze around sharply as Brand crossed the space between his lookout spot and the truck. He climbed into the cab and started the motor but didn't turn on the lights.

"We'll move closer to the end of the canyon since it's about time for Ward and Milt to reconnoiter."

Perhaps a quarter of a mile from their original post, he stopped. "There they are," he said.

She squinted. A barely visible dark shape came toward them. "I don't see how you can tell who it is," she whispered.

"Your eyes get used to the shadows after a while."

The car drew near and stopped. "Nothing, Brand," Milt said softly. "There's a helicopter to the north of us. Is that part of the surveillance?"

"That's General Montague. You don't think he'd sit home and bite his nails while we have all the fun, do you?"

She heard low laughter from the other car and then it pulled away. She drew in a sharp breath.

"Go to that bunch of salt cedars over there, Beth," Brand instructed. "I'll wait here."

Sliding down the slight embankment behind the ragged bushes, Beth checked her gun in the holster and hunched down to wait. After what seemed hours, Brand drove toward her and she went to meet him.

"It's four o'clock, Beth. We'll drive up the highway a

few miles and see if Ward has seen a signal from the helicopter. Must have been a false alarm or the look-outs learned we'd be here."

Thankfully, she climbed into the truck and a few minutes later, car lights blinked on and off twice ahead of them. They stopped as the car drew alongside them.

"They called it off, Brand," Milt said. "One of the agents out of Sonoita came by and said the trucks have already gone through without any trouble."

"Okay. You may as well go on home, then. We'll see you next week for the desert training."

They separated and Brand turned the truck toward Nogales and Beth relaxed, conscious of a feeling of let-down. Better than blown up, she decided, and let her breath out audibly.

"This is a lot of what goes on out here, Beth. The buildup for the big job that never comes off. Then the blowup when you aren't expecting it. That means you stay alert at all times and never—*never*—let down your guard."

As they reached the office, he said, "Desert survival training is every night next week. Get plenty of rest tomorrow and I'll see you Monday." He hesitated, then asked, "Do you need any help shopping for gro-ceries?"

"I can manage," she said dryly. She was being turned loose on her own in a hurry. Not that she needed his support, but she had supposed...

"Be careful, Beth," he warned again.

She nodded as she slid from the truck, taking her pack from beneath the seat. "Good night, Brand." It was morning, but it didn't matter. She was tired enough for it to be night and she was ready for some sleep. The trip across country plus the uneventful night watch was catching up with her.

SHE FOUND A TRACK at a YMCA branch only a few blocks from her and ran early Sunday morning before the sun got too warm. September days in Arizona were still hot, Brand told her, even though the nights were cool.

In downtown Nogales, she found a small grocery store open and bought a few groceries. There were some cooking utensils in the trailer but no coffeepot. She bought a small one and couldn't wait to get back to try it out. Standing in the checkout line, she listened to the conversations around her, all in Spanish, which she understood easily.

She answered the checkout girl's "*Buenas tardes*" with "Hello" and a smile, automatically counting her change along with the girl: *uno, dos, tres.*

As she drove back to the office she saw that Alfredo's truck was parked in front, but there was no one at Brand's trailer. She shrugged and went in to unpack her groceries.

Perking coffee sent a pleasant fragrance through the rooms and she sat at the counter, staring through the front window at the foreign Arizona landscape. Last night they had been lucky. No dangerous confrontation as they expected, but next time—tomorrow, the day after—it might be different.

But the feelings inside of her had changed. She no longer felt unsure of herself; she no longer wondered if she was doing the right thing. Brand was putting her on her own, telling her she was responsible for him as well as for herself. She felt his withdrawal from her, not knowing if he were a friend or an enemy. Neither. He was her supervisor; she was his partner. That looked like the way he wanted it and she would go along with him.

Finishing her light lunch and coffee, she took clothes to the laundromat she had spotted on her shopping trip. Stopped for a stoplight, she let her gaze roam over the sun-drenched buildings, one marked as a museum, probably not open on Sundays. The clock on the domed tower was stopped at six thirteen and she tried to imagine if it was significant of some happening or if it quit running at that time on its own.

The lights changed and her musings went to Brand. She straightened against the velour seat of the little car; her thoughts had a way of going in circles until they reached her supervisor.

Watch it, Beth. You could become really attached to your partner and all he wants from you is dependability to do the job at hand.

Dusk fell without her seeing another person and she spent the time writing letters, then went outside to watch the sun set behind what her maps and brochures said were the Sierrita Mountains. It was as fabulous a vista as the one viewed from Cattleman's Steakhouse.

In bed early she lay awake thinking about recent events, wondering what lay ahead, knowing it was foolish to do so. It was a job you learned as you went, taking orders, doing whatever was required to put the area in the safety zone for its inhabitants.

Since telling her about his friend's death, Brand had never mentioned it again except when talking to her parents, but she was sure it was always there in his mind. Just as the thought of Jud was always in hers.

Chapter Seven

Her initiation into the art of desert survival was just that: learning to survive. Paired with Brand against Milt and Ward with Alfredo as umpire, they spent the night in the desert. Across dry riverbeds and arroyos they chased and were chased, finally capturing Milt as Ward escaped across the Mexican border. They regrouped at the office to discuss Alfredo's report on their escapade. It was seven thirty in the morning.

Beth was exhausted and sure half the sand from the dunes filled her clothing, especially her panties. The fine gravel ground into her hips and thighs and she breathed a sigh of relief when Brand dismissed them for the day.

"We're going for breakfast, Beth," he said. "Are you ready to eat?"

In the process of unpinning her hair she had stuck under the fatigue cap, she shook her head.

"No thanks. Wake me in time to go to work."

She didn't look at either of the men as she left the office, running easily across the gravel yard back to number ten. Undressing, she rolled her fatigues so she could shake the sand from them later, stepped into the shower and turned the water on full force—which wasn't much.

Drying, she stretched to limber her stiffened body. She really should run, she thought, but instead she slipped a short cotton gown over her head, went to bed, and was asleep within seconds.

THE WEEK PASSED in a haze of work, hide-and-seek in the desert, and briefings. She analyzed problems best after sleeping and made it a habit to lie in bed, eyes closed, going over what they had done the night before. When Brand shot questions at her, she was ready.

On Saturday morning, Ward and Milt got ready to return to their operations base at Lukeville.

No one had mentioned the fact that she had kept up with the men in the desert where they were trained and she was not. They expected her to do her job and she felt justified in thinking she had done quite well. A couple of times she had looked up to find Brand's eyes on her, but they were dark and told her nothing.

She stood now watching as Ward and Milt loaded their truck and got ready to move out. Ward put his hand out to her and she took it:

He looked her over and turned to Brand. "If you'd like to switch partners, I'd consider it," he said.

Brand shook his head. "I can't find you in the desert now. If you had Beth, you'd disappear forever."

Ward laughed but Beth, standing to one side, looked to see that Brand was not smiling. She stiffened, uneasy about the brief exchange without knowing why.

As the truck pulled away, she started toward her trailer. "Do you have plans for the weekend?" Brand asked.

"Yes, I'm going to sleep," she told him.

"A good idea. We'll be patrolling days next week." He watched Beth walk away before he went into the office.

Apparently Brand had dismissed her from his everyday life away from the Patrol as if she had never been a part of it. Perhaps she hadn't. Somehow she missed the kisses that hadn't seemed all that casual to her. She had obviously read something into them that Brand had never intended. Once convinced that she wouldn't change her mind about the Patrol, he dropped any pretense of trying to make love to her. Only to herself would she admit it left an empty feeling within her slim body.

Pressing her lips together to prevent a sudden trembling, she went home.

Saturday was a lost cause. She took care of her laundry, cleaned the gritty dust from the trailer, ate a thick bacon and egg sandwich, and fell into bed at five o'clock, waking at five on Sunday morning.

A thin trickle of cool water from the shower revived her and she sat with coffee thinking of her first week in Nogales.

As far as she was concerned, it wasn't too bad, but Brand wasn't one to dish out much praise. Criticism, yes; constructive, she admitted. But aside from the shortened lookout for the terrorists' reported attempt to hijack the nuclear convoy, there was little to judge her performance on. Perhaps there never would be a test of her abilities in a dangerous situation—if she was lucky.

She sighed and put on her warm-up suit to run. Late September mornings were getting too cool for shorts. Outside, the quietness surrounded her. The sky was cloudless and blue. Two runners were ahead of her on the track and she trotted along the inside letting her mind go blank and the leftover tension disappeared from her body.

Back in the trailer, she settled down to write letters home and to Smitty. "I like my job, Smitty, but Brand Page is the same as when we were at school—solemnly dedicated to his job. He seems to have accepted me, but aside from issuing instructions, he has little to do with me and I never see him unless we're on duty." Smitty would answer that she was lucky, at that, Beth concluded, smiling as she sealed the letter.

She drove downtown to the post office, dropped the letters, and made a circle to return home. Downtown Nogales was bustling with tourists, identified by their clothing, and Mexican nationals, identified by car licence plates and shopping bags filled with goods that were in short supply across the border.

It was after one o'clock when she reentered the trailer and her stomach was beginning to notice that she hadn't eaten. In her meager supply of food was some hamburger she had made into patties and frozen.

She removed one from the freezer and placed it in the frying pan to cook while she arranged a slice of cheese, tomato and onion on a plate, reaching for the jalapeño peppers she had developed a taste for. It was useless to buy bread for one person so, when her burger was cooked to her satisfaction, she took a Seven-Up, sat down at the breakfast bar and enjoyed her meal without bread.

Feet propped on the stool opposite her, she stared dreamily into space. The unfamiliar ring of the phone on the counter nearby startled her. It rang a second time and she reached for it.

"Page."

"I thought perhaps you planned to sleep all day," Brand said.

"I have that idea in mind."

"Too late," he said. "Be ready in fifteen minutes."

She hung up the phone. *You can't reach here from your ranch in fifteen minutes,* she thought, *so where are you?*

Brand had never mentioned a girl friend but she assumed he had one. An eligible bachelor like him couldn't run around loose forever. She didn't pursue the thought; it was none of her business. She was his partner in the Patrol—period.

Pulling out the survival pack she kept ready, she changed into fatigues and the boots she had bought at Brand's suggestion, and put a change of jeans and underthings in the flat briefcase that fit under the truck seat. She brushed her teeth, pushed her hair up and pinned it to fit under her hat, closed the window in her bedroom and was ready when the horn blasted outside.

Locking the door behind her, she climbed into the truck cab, reaching to put her things back of the seat. Only then did she glance at Brand.

"You look tired," he said.

"I am."

He watched her a moment longer before turning the truck around. She didn't ask where they were going; it didn't matter. Wherever it was, there would be sand and mesquite, desert squirrels and jackrabbits.

At the airport, he turned down the faint tracks. She was quiet as they bumped along, waiting to see if he would tell her anything about the problem they faced.

Past the airport property, he turned right into the Tumacacori Mountains, following the faint trail on a southwesterly course that went into the Atascosa Hills. Their first week of training hadn't brought them to this area and the wildness of the completely uninhabited land brought her upright in the seat. Somehow, she expected a signpost saying "City Limits: Hell—Elev: 10,000 feet below sea level."

She glanced at Brand's face which told her exactly what she expected—nothing.

A row of smoke bushes and small water oaks ringed a low mound, and Brand guided the truck to it, pulling into the scant cover provided by the growth. It would be shaded in a few minutes as the sun dropped behind the mountains.

"Beth."

Feet braced against the truck floor, she turned to look at him. He unfastened his seat belt and reached for her, and her eyes widened in surprise as she sat stiffly within the confines of her own seat belt. His fingers along her jaw held her face still as he bent to place his mouth on hers.

As their lips met, he whispered, "Kiss me, Beth."

Eyes wide open, she saw the ring of lashes, the gray in his brows more bristly than the darker hairs, the smooth pores of his tanned skin. As her lids drooped her lips parted and her head relaxed on the truck seat. He slid one arm around her, pulling her against him, straining the seat belt, and her fatigue cap tumbled from her head. Both his hands moved, feeling her outline through the stiffness of the fatigues she had chosen to wear.

He wore jeans and she had no trouble finding his hard thighs, caressing upward across him. The seat belt loosened as he found the catch and pulled her body into the shape of his. Waves of warmth swept through her as she obeyed his demand, kissing him with seeking mouth, fingers gripping his shirt front.

When his lips freed hers, she opened her eyes to gaze into stormy gray pools above her as he let her go, hand sliding down her arms to pull her hands away from him.

He shook his head. "I didn't bring you here for that."

Beth didn't answer but turned away, staring without sight into the shadows around them, listening as he explained why he had brought her.

"Information came through that questionable cargo moved through the Mexican Sierras Friday night coming in this direction." He opened the door on his side. "They may turn west before they reach our area, but we have to be on the lookout." He got out, looking back at her.

"I'll be in that grove of oaks over by that wash. If you hear any sound you can't identify, whistle." His outline showed briefly in front of the truck before he disappeared into a shallow wash.

She picked up her cap, replaced it on her head, and got out of the truck. Her legs were trembling from the avalanche of feeling unearthed by the unexpected kiss, leaving her wondering what had happened to her usual common sense. If she fell in love with Brand, she was in for trouble judging by his indifference to her.

If? She stared into the semidarkness. The emptiness when Brand removed his arms from around her; the jelly that replaced the muscles in her legs; the lonely aching in her chest—all attested to the fact that she was already beyond saving. Her self-discipline was going to be put to a stringent test starting right now.

Minutes passed and she ran his comments back through her mind like the replay of a tape. It sounded odd. Someone walked through the Mexican Sierras Friday night? Or did he say walking? Forty-eight hours ago. Uneasiness stirred through her and she squinted in the half-light.

Twilight brought a decided drop in the desert temperature and she shivered. Moving away from the truck, she went on all fours to get to the low bushes, making her way down the wash left by flash floods that came out of the mountains every spring and fall.

Thinking she heard voices, she stopped. The sound faded, only to become clearer a few feet from her around a bend in the shallow ditch she was following.

"Stay by the truck," Brand had said. She turned to make sure it was still in sight and started to move on when she heard his voice. His voice and others—all in Spanish.

She held her breath, listening in disbelief as the discussion continued. They had set her up.

Damn you, Brandon Page, she thought, anger shooting through her body.

Unfastening the flap on her holster, she withdrew her gun, backing away from her listening post, moving noiselessly up the slight incline past the spot the men occupied. She lay flat where she could look down at them.

A million stars and half a moon illumined the desert landscape and her eyes, accustomed to the half-light, could distinguish outlines enough for identification. Brand's arms were tied behind him and Ward's .357 Magnum was aimed at his chest. Milt sat in the dimness to one side.

The whispering desert wind covered her next move and Ward stiffened as the cold barrel of her gun touched his temple.

"*Mueve y estas muerto,*" she told him in softly drawled Spanish, translating it into English, "Move and you're dead."

She reached, taking his gun and slinging it away from him, knowing it would fill with sand and he'd spend hours cleaning it. She stepped back, hoping he would grab for her; she was ready to crown him with the gun.

Instead, he swore. "What the hell?"

"It could have been worse—I could have pulled a purely feminine trick and become unhinged due to worry over my boss and shot first." Her voice was husky with anger. "It was a rotten trick."

Brand said quietly, "We needed to know how you might react, Beth. The boys we're looking for play for keeps."

"You could all be dead," she told him, still shaking with anger.

"We aren't," he said as Milt untied him.

"How well do you speak Spanish, Beth?" Ward asked.

"I taught it for several years," she said.

"You knew, Brand?"

Brand nodded. "You weren't the only one operating without full knowledge, Beth. Sometimes it's better that way." He stood up. "Intelligence tells us that the big drug smugglers are lying low because of a leak by informants. It will probably be a few weeks before they surface again." He turned to Ward. "I'll be in touch with you."

They shook hands and Ward turned to Beth, his teeth flashing. "Glad you're on our side," and held out his hand. She glared a moment before she accepted it. He went to retrieve his gun.

Milt took the fatigue cap from her head, bent and kissed the topknot of hair, replacing the cap. "Me too." He and Ward left, walking down the arroyo away from them.

Beth ran up the bank ahead of Brand, reaching the truck and swinging up into the seat before he got there. He started the motor, pulling away from the tree cover before he turned on his lights.

As he turned right on I-19, he asked, "Are you hungry?"

"Yes," she said.

"Will Letty's do?" he asked, naming a popular Mexican café not far from them.

"Does she make good cheeseburgers?"

He laughed. "No. Try the steak tampiqueño."

"All right." She unbuttoned her fatigue shirt and pulled it off, disclosing her Atlanta Braves T-shirt. She jammed the fatigue cap that would roll up without wrinkling into the pocket of her shirt and stuck them behind the seat, reaching to loosen the pins from her hair and shake it loose.

Parking the truck in the well-occupied area near the café, he turned to look at her. "Are you going to sulk?"

"I'm too mad to sulk. I want you to know without any doubt that I think it was a cheap shot, testing me, or not. I'm already aware that you don't really trust me, Brand, and you can remember the one instance of my freezing forever if that's what you want to do." Her ground-together teeth chopped the drawl short. "Trust your training, Brand; you've done a good job on me."

A finger lifted her chin as he met her anger. He smiled, brushing her lips with his fingertip before he opened his door to slide out and come around to her side. They walked without touching into the crowded café.

Beth let him order the steak he recommended and ate in silence when Letty, the café owner they all knew, brought their dinners. She chatted with Brand in mixed English and Spanish which Beth understood without any trouble.

"Did you and Dolores patch up your quarrel?" Letty asked him.

A muscle twitched in his jaw as he nodded. "Yes."

As Letty turned to her other customers, Beth concentrated on her meal. Dolores? One of the secretaries

from headquarters was named Dolores, but she had no
idea if that was the one. It was a common name among
the local population.

Finishing her plate of the tasty Mexican steak, she
leaned back in the booth as exhaustion spread through-
out her body. Her lids were heavy as she looked across
at Brand.

"There'll be briefings two days next week from a
representative of the Drug Enforcement Administration. Attendance is mandatory. Other than those days,
we'll shorten our hours; we more than make up for it
when we're working a problem."

Brand stood up, taking their check to the cashier. She
followed him, looking up to meet the dark eyes of the
Dolores from headquarters.

She smiled at Brand. "Looks like you two have been
in the boondocks again."

Was there more than a friendly question there? Beth
couldn't tell but her lips tightened. *I'm not your competi-
tion if that's worrying you*, she thought, and wondered at
the empty feeling that went with the thought, remembering the kiss not many hours ago.

Brand gave Dolores a smile in return. "Only in the
best part of town."

"Will you be around next week?"

He nodded. "Most of it. We have the briefing with
DEA."

Dolores smiled a distant smile at Beth and turned
fully toward Brand. "I'll see you then." Her long
fingers with perfectly shaped nails touched his arm as
she gave him an intimate smile.

Beth moved to stand by the door, clenching her

hands, drawing attention to her own stubby nails that broke every time she fired her pistol.

"Sorry," Brand apologized a moment later as he joined her. She didn't answer him, having no idea why he should be sorry.

In the truck, he asked, "What do you hear from home, Beth?"

"One letter since I called them. There's been a delay in the delivery of Dad's van—it'll be another four to eight weeks. I guess that'll make it a nice Christmas present for them."

"Are you homesick?" The question was unexpected.

She thought about it. "Yes, a little."

Brand's hand left the wheel to cover hers where it lay on her thigh. He squeezed it and took his hand away. A few minutes later, he pulled into the driveway by the office, took his gun from behind the seat and came around to help her out with her equipment and gun. She placed her key in his outstretched hand and walked past him as he opened the door.

"Get some of our reading material from Alfredo tomorrow morning and familiarize yourself with our basic formula for different types of surveillances. I'll be at headquarters most of the day."

She nodded.

"Good night, Beth." He turned and left. Beth locked the door behind him, feeling as if she'd been dismissed like a good little girl.

Chapter Eight

She studied; she ran her five miles, and one afternoon she drove downtown and parked in the Customs Building parking lot near the Mexico-U.S. border and walked through the turnstile into Nogales, Mexico.

Small barefoot children met her with outstretched hands, begging. A blind man held a cup on the corner. Another, without legs, sat against a building sheltered from the wind that had turned cold.

Beth put money in the grubby little hands, the cup, and the tattered hat the legless man held. Then she turned into a side street where there was little traffic of any kind, pedestrian or motorized.

Stopping at a cracked, dusty window, she gazed in at the intricate designs on leather goods: saddles, handbags, knife cases. A fly-speckled sign read "Open" and she pushed the creaky door open to walk inside. In the dim interior she stood looking around until a soft voice spoke from a corner.

"*Buenas tardes, señorita.*"

She blinked and saw the man sitting behind a littered

table working on a saddle. She touched the detailed work. "*Buenas tardes, señor. Es bonito.*"

"*Gracias.*" He swept his hand outward and tried his English. "Look?"

She nodded and walked through the cluttered store, leaving with a gorgeous light-tan leather and suede bag for Mary Ann, a knife with tooled case and a set of old intricately detailed spurs for Jim. She haggled over the price with the man as tourists are supposed to do, giving more than he asked and considered it a great bargain. He grinned all the time after he learned she spoke Spanish, intrigued by her ability to turn off the southern drawl and effect a more Latin one.

At another store down the street, she found a hand-embroidered tablecloth for Mary Ann and a turquoise necklace with matching earrings for Smitty, and turned back toward the Customs Building that had remained in her sight except in the leather shop.

As she crossed into the United States, she spotted a Kresge store and, sure enough, they already had Christmas paper out. She grinned at the outright commercialism of Americans and went home with her Christmas shopping complete.

THE DEA BRIEFINGS started at one on Thursday and she was fine until the movies late Friday afternoon. The film showed a raid with graphic pictures and colors involving prostitutes, illegal aliens and innocent bystanders. She left alone through a back door of the building and was able to reach her trailer before she became violently ill.

"Remember this peaceful scene," Brand had told

her as he kissed her by the ocean. "You won't see it again." He was right. Peaceful scenes from the civilized world disappeared in the land of greedy criminals.

Jud's work. Brand's work. Her work. How much could they hope to accomplish outnumbered a hundred to one by people who schemed with cold-blooded skill against the unwary?

The room grew dark and still she sat, wondering why anyone stayed with an outfit that fought an unending battle with very little reward. What was she doing here?

The strident ring of the phone didn't even startle her as deeply as she was immersed in the dark questions pounding at her. Her movements were slow as she moved to pick up the receiver.

"Beth?" Brand's sharp inquiry before she had time to identify herself brought her up short.

"Yes."

"Were you asleep?" The query this time seemed more gentle.

"No."

"I'll be over in a moment." He hung up.

Not "May I come over?" Just "I'll be over."

"Come over to see me, why don't you, Brand?" she said to the dead connection. Her hand still rested on the receiver when he knocked on the door and, though he turned the knob, it didn't open. She had learned to lock a door—any door—the minute she went through it if she didn't intend to go back through it within a second.

As she opened the door for him, he stepped through, and she was suddenly chilled at the stern look on his face. Now what?

He didn't make her wait for the news. "The last part of the briefing for the supervisors gave us a set of orders," he said, taking in the tenseness in the slim body leaning against the breakfast bar as she faced him.

He crossed to stand near her, then sat down on the stool at the end of the counter. "Do you remember the friend I told you got caught in the wrong place and killed?"

She nodded, swallowing over the dryness in her throat. His mouth tightened in the controlled angry look that went with the clenched fists on the counter in front of him.

"Special agents made a sweep along the border between El Paso and Columbus, New Mexico, and rounded up a group smuggling illegal aliens across from Central Mexico." He waited a moment before continuing but she made no comment.

"Among the organizers of the group was a man involved in the killing. His name is Varro, well known along the border for all his illegal operations and criminal connections in North and South America.

"How could you tell that after all this time?" she asked.

"Some of the poor devils being smuggled across had paid him their life's savings for a guaranteed safe trip to Denver and when the agents closed in on them, he disappeared. They gave us a lot of information it would have taken us years to get. Along with the information of his route up through Mexico, they had a map of alternate directions he planned to take in case he was discovered."

"Surely he wouldn't be foolish enough to stick to those routes after they were picked up."

"He doesn't know they have the maps; they stole them while he was drunk and made copies, then returned them."

"Honor among thieves?"

His expression softened. "You can't blame them for trying to get some place they might survive with a little more decency, Beth."

Surprised at his defense of the aliens, she said, doubtfully, "No, of course not." She had no idea how far she would go to change her status in life if everything was as hopeless as she knew some of their lives were. No, she couldn't blame them.

He drew in a deep breath and went on. "The agents are still working the New Mexico-Arizona border with another patrol between Douglas and Naco, Arizona. You and I will take over from there back to Duquesne and Harshaw."

He lifted his gaze to meet her stare. "It's partly on my property; partly on Nash's property. There are a lot of hiding places in that area: old mines, old ghost towns with caves and crevices it would take weeks to go through."

"Do you think he'll take a chance knowing you might be waiting for him?"

"I don't know. We can't afford to wait and see." He stood up. "Be ready to leave in half an hour. Take a change of clothing."

With the rotten taste still in her mouth from the afternoon movies, she scrubbed her teeth and rinsed her mouth, tucking a pair of jeans and flannel shirt into the briefcase she usually carried and was ready when the single horn blast sounded. Checking to see that everything was cut off and locked, she ran to the truck, climbing into the seat beside Brand to fasten the seat belt all in the same movement.

He drove silently and she knew he was thinking of the reason they sat together as partners in the unmarked Customs truck. Each of them had lost a loved one to someone similar to the man they hunted together. What would he do differently if he had a man as a partner? She didn't ask, following her own thoughts as Brand followed his.

They changed direction and she looked up to see a sign that said: Patagonia, 12 miles. Patagonia, Brand's hometown.

"Do we go close to your home on our way?" she asked.

"Yes. We're going to stay there tonight," he said and she turned sharply to look at him in the dim light from the dash.

"The stakeout doesn't begin tonight?"

"The quarry hasn't left Agua Prieto yet."

She frowned. "That's across from Douglas."

"Yes. We can't do anything as long as he's on Mexican soil."

The truck headlights picked out a big sprawling adobe-and-log house as they went up an incline and around a mesa perhaps fifty feet high and a quarter mile long. The house sat in a grove of the biggest water oaks she had seen since she arrived in Arizona. In the outline of the headlights, she couldn't tell how big the house was, but it covered a lot of ground.

As she slid from the truck, she smelled a familiar fragrance. Brand came around to where she stood and she asked, "Magnolias?"

His teeth flashed white in the darkness. "Arizona is a strange land of contrasts, Beth, and unless you abide by her rules, can be very hostile and dangerous."

I know about hostility, she thought, thinking of the coolness she had lived with for weeks now.

He touched her arm. "I guess Luis and Aurelia haven't gotten back from Tucson, but they should be back before too late. They live with me and take care of the place."

Taking her things from beneath the seat, she turned to walk with him up the back steps and across a wide porch. He paused to flip a light switch before they entered a big country kitchen.

"Are you hungry?" he asked.

Beth was busy looking around at Brand's home, answering him with a shake of her head. Her stomach remembered the movies and their reasons for being there and she had no desire for food.

"I'll show you where to put your things."

She followed him across a hallway to an open door and when he turned on the light, she stared. A huge four-poster bed, reminiscent of her great-grandmother's in Savannah, dominated the room. A bright red-and-white quilt covered it.

"It's beautiful," she said.

"My parents' room," he said. "My mother made the quilt before you were born." He turned back to meet her questioning eyes and smiled. "They've been dead for many years, Beth. It's all right."

He stood close to her, one finger tilting her chin. "Are you ready for bed or would you like to have a drink?"

"I'm not tired," she said, feeling the quiver go from the tips of his fingers to her toes.

He continued to hold her chin upward and bent to place his mouth on hers. She held herself still, trying to ignore the stirrings inside her, but as the pressure on her lips increased, she stood on tiptoe, her hands at his waist. He pulled her against him, their bodies aligned, gently forcing her lips apart. Shadows of multicolored warmth spread through her. When he had parted her lips to his satisfaction, he lifted his mouth to bite into the softness, moving to her chin, feathery kisses stroking her throat. Tracing past her ear to her hairline, his kisses triggered warm shivers through her body and her breath caught.

"Brand?" She turned her face into his shoulder, holding tightly to him.

"Welcome to Patagonia, Beth," he said softly. His hold on her lightened and he was looking down at her, eyes hidden by his dark lashes. "Let's get that drink."

The living room was big with a vaulted ceiling and the coolness was welcome against her hot cheeks. Brand left her by the mantel and went to a small wet bar at the side of the room. Like the other furniture in the room, it was oak, with a double stainless-steel sink hidden until he slid a top back.

"How about a margarita?" he asked.

"Like the one we had at Cattleman's?"

"You'll probably like the strawberry ones I make even better than those."

"I'm willing to take the chance," she said.

He measured and mixed and put the ingredients into the blender holding up the results for her to see. "It's pretty," she said as he handed her a frosted glass. She sipped. "It's even more delicious than my first one. Must be the strawberries."

He crossed the room to sit on the hearth in front of her as she sat on a big hassock. He glanced at his watch. "I expected Luis back by now."

"Do they ever stay all night when they go shopping?" she asked.

"No, not usually." As he put his drink beside him on the bricks the telephone on the bar rang and he went to answer it.

"Page here," he said, his eyes on Beth as she ran her finger around the edge of her glass and licked it, looking up to meet his gaze and smiling at him.

He listened for a moment and said, "All right, Luis. Don't worry about it. I'll be here tonight, but I'll be gone when you get home." He spoke in Spanish.

He hung up the phone and came back to sit on the hearth. "Luis has car trouble and they won't be back tonight." He smiled. "I guess you'll have to do without a chaperone."

She smiled back at him. "One more of your margaritas and you'll be absolutely safe."

"I will," he said softly. "What about you?"

"I'll let you worry about that," she said after a moment of meeting his look.

"That's quite a responsibility," he said. "Let's try the second drink and see what happens."

As he took her glass, she stood up and moved to the

two-cushioned loveseat running her hands over the smooth material as she sat down. She was suddenly tired and put her head back, eyes closed. When the cushions moved with Brand's weight, Beth opened her eyes and smiled, watching as his face lowered to hers and their lips met. He was holding a glass in each hand so only his mouth touched hers. She kept her hands by her side, her heartbeat surging in her chest, spreading warmth through her body.

He lifted his head, lips curved in a smile, lashes hiding his eyes, and brought a glass around to give her. Her breathing was unsteady as she touched her lips to the glass, sipping the cool drink. A piece of strawberry went in her mouth and she bit into it, feeling the seeds between her teeth. Her body was warm and relaxed and it was an effort to keep her eyes open. She stirred and moved closer to Brand as he took the glass from her and his arm went around her.

"Beth," he whispered.

She wanted to ask what had brought about the change in him that made him want to kiss her after all this time, but no words would come. Her head slid back on his shoulder and her eyes opened wide for an instant.

"It's your responsibility," she said and feathery black lashes closed to lie against the faint circles beneath her eyes.

A strand of silvery hair caught on the pocket button of his shirt and he untangled it, smoothing it back. She murmured in her sleep and turned to press her head into the curve of his shoulder. He held her there as she slept, feeling her steady heartbeat beneath his hand. It was a long time before he shifted to get his hand under her legs to lift her from the couch. She didn't stir as he carried her to the bedroom where they had taken her things earlier.

Placing her on the bright quilt, he slipped off the plain cowboy boots. She lay quiet, her face turned toward him as he unbuttoned the white blouse, a spot of pink on the collar where a piece of the strawberry had fallen. He unfastened her belt, loosening it enough so that when he unzipped the jeans, they slid off easily over her hips as he raised them.

He stood up, smiling at the quiet form on the bed. The margaritas proved a bit too much for her on an empty stomach and a good night's sleep would do her a world of good. Heaven only knew when she'd get the next one.

Turning back the quilt, he moved her onto the cool sheets, eyes going from her closed ones to the small breasts held by the lacy cup of her bra, to her flat stomach covered by thin white panties, leaving the outline of her body plainly visible.

He touched her thigh with two fingers, feeling the firmness beneath the smooth skin. She was lightly tanned on all exposed areas of her body. He resisted the urge to continue, drew the sheet up over her and went to the door, looking back at her still form as he turned off the light.

Chapter Nine

Back in the living room Brand prowled restlessly, finally going to the wide front window and pulling the draperies, turning the lights off to gaze across the expanse of desert by the end of the mesa that edged the yard. Somewhere behind the ridge of the Santa Rita Mountains lightning played, but from experience he knew rain would not reach them. Not likely. It would fall in the nine-thousand-foot range of mountains and wash over the sparsely covered crumbling limestone to become a rolling flash flood in the lower area. Small benefit would be gained by anyone from the much-needed rains and the ranchers in the area would have sense enough to stay out of the flash-flood zones until the water roared its strength away in the thirsty desert.

His gaze rested on the dark sky that covered the southern portion of his ranch where they would be going to look for Varro. Even the name caused his blood to run cold. Ruthless, cunning, desperate for money and power. He would be taking Beth into the wildness of the desert he had warned her about repeatedly. Yes, she was trained. Yes, she was capable. No, he didn't want her in this outfit with him.

Beth Page. *My God, what am I going to do with her*? He knew what he wanted to do but common sense and a fierce sense of loyalty to the organization they belonged to forbade it. He knew the first time he heard her name and saw her that she would be trouble.

The letter from Herb Crosley, his supervisor in Nogales before he quit Customs, now a big shot director in Washington, came his second day of classes in Glynco, Georgia. When he agreed to sign back up in the Customs Patrol where he had previously spent six years, Herb asked him to go back to Glynco for a supervisory refresher course.

"You'll be about all there is now, Brand, maybe one more officer plus an administrator, but with all the cutbacks, I doubt you'll be assigned any more."

"I don't mind, Herb. I prefer a small force. As long as we get cooperation from Lukeville when trouble is too big for us."

"And it might get that way, Brand, you know. The criminals above and below our southwestern borders are smart and just waiting to find the opening they need to start illegal deals in God-knows-what kind of traffic."

Yes, he knew their modus operandi. He had seen it all—murder, smuggling, robbery, kidnapping—you name it, he had seen it all. That had been his reason for quitting the Patrol two years before. When his lifelong friend and neighbor, Nash Travis, was murdered in cold blood for no reason, he vowed to get his killers somehow. Herb's offer to give him Nogales as his headquarters presented the opportunity.

He didn't know or care about Herb's ulterior motives—not then, he didn't. His mouth twisted along with an uncertain faltering of his heartbeat as his thoughts went back to Beth Page.

The letter explained Herb's plan quite well.

"In the advance class where you'll be sitting in, there's a woman that shows a lot of promise toward making a good Patrol officer. There are only two in the class and the one I refer to is Beth Page. No relation to you, of course, Brand. She's fluent in Spanish and French. We don't need the French right now, but the Spanish is a definite plus in your area. She's your other officer and I want you to pay close attention to her as the course progresses. If she falls on her face, we'll look somewhere else, but from her past-experience résumé, her physical performances, and determination, I think she's the one for you."

You think, Herb? What about what I think?

He turned away from the window, leaving the drapes open, and sat in the dark thinking that he should have followed his first inclination right then and told Herb what he could do with the Patrol and Beth Page. His hesitation was costing him dearly.

"It wasn't in the résumé," Herb's letter went on, "but during her background investigation, we found that Beth's fiancé was Judson Chambers. Remember him? He was the one killed in that big raid in Miami a year ago. He not only organized and tracked the masterminds behind the deal, but he gave his life when it became necessary to save his teammates."

Brand remembered. The seething inside of him was still there when Nash was killed. Money to back up their people and the activities that would net them more of the criminals was short, and in cutting back the government set them up to lose more good people. Fighting with all the reasoning he could summon, he steered clear of any contact with former officers, not wanting to hear the same story he had heard for years. Not enough money; not enough good men; not enough backing; not enough of anything.

When Herb called him, he was ready. Whatever he could do, he would do it, and one day—*one day*—he would meet the ones who were responsible for Nash's death, sure that they were guilty of even more heinous crimes along the way.

He hadn't counted on Beth Page.

She wasn't hard to spot. Of the two females in a class of fifty, she couldn't be missed. Silvery blond hair swung in heavy waves almost to her shoulders. Her light gray eyes, almost the same color as her hair, seemed to gaze into scenes that he didn't see in the classroom. Fringed by feathery charcoal lashes, a sort of tenderness shown through, as though she were looking at something or someone she loved. It was a strange feeling to look straight at her and know she didn't see you.

He watched her run track on days no one else would; out early before classes, out late after classes, she ran. Often he wondered if she ran from memories of Judson Chambers. She went to classes, she ate in the cafeteria; she talked to Carol Smith, Smitty to everyone, her roommate. He had watched fellow officers approach her to ask for dates and see them smilingly turned down.

He was filled with resentment at having her assigned to him without even a by-your-leave. He did not want a woman. The Patrol, to his notion, was not the place for a woman and he did not classify that thought as prejudice. It was a rugged, rough, fighting outfit, not designed for the gentleness of a woman. Sure, there were women who could qualify, Beth Page among them, but qualifying and doing the job were two decidedly different things.

He made it a point to run into her at the cafeteria early one morning just after she completed her turns around the track. Although they were among a very few people eating breakfast, he approached her table.

"May I sit with you?" he asked.

Wide gray eyes lifted to his face and, before she spoke, her glance went around the near-empty room.

"Yes, of course," she said after a moment. His smile was uncontrollable as he listened to the softness of her drawl. Some southerners were hard to understand, but not Beth. She spoke clearly but the drawl was unmistakable.

As he sat opposite her, she looked him over deliberately, taking in his dark hair, generously sprinkled with gray, his thin face and, as he smiled at her, the square white teeth behind a wide firm mouth.

Without a word, she went back to her meal.

"Will that hold you till lunch?" he asked indicating the light meal on her plate.

"Yes. I'll take some fruit back with me."

He leaned his elbows on the table, ignoring his own food. "Do you know your assignment?"

She looked up with an interested gleam in her eyes.

"I thought we got our assignments later after quotas were announced for the regions."

"Sometimes they promise assignments to get you to enlist in the Patrol if you have the qualifications." He let his eyes go over her deliberately and she stiffened.

"I wasn't promised an assignment. Perhaps I don't have the right qualifications."

"Are you bilingual?"

The wide gray eyes narrowed, and for a moment he thought she wouldn't answer him, giving the appearance that the question angered her. "I speak French and Spanish fluently with a smidgen of English thrown in," she said, her soft drawl sharpened to cut the words off.

He grinned. "Your accent certainly gives English a whole different sound."

She gave him a studied look and went back to eating.

"I wasn't being critical. Your accent is intriguing to say the least."

Finishing her meal in silence, she picked up her tray and left it on another stack, taking an apple from the counter as she passed it. He fell into step with her outside the cafeteria doors but a sudden rainstorm caused them to have to run for the barracks and he was forced to postpone his questions to another time.

It was unusual to find someone in the class with the same last name as well as the first initial. Their papers were mixed several times and he always looked at any of hers that ended up in his hands. She was very near the top of the class academically, well qualified in shooting, tops in the calisthenics, thoroughly indoctrinated in the regulations.

The more he saw of Beth Page, the less he wanted her as his partner in the wilds of Arizona. Raised in gentler circumstances than she would ever find out west, he wondered what he'd do with her when they stayed four days in the one hundred plus temperatures in the desert, hiding behind mesquite bushes and dodging rattlesnakes. Snakes of all kinds. He determined to promise her anything to keep her from going. He wrote a letter to Herb, begging him to reconsider.

"She's everything you said, Herb, but she's a woman. All right—let N.O.W. have a ball with that statement, but before you listen to them, listen to me. Send the leader of that powerful lobby to Sasabe, to Lukeville, to Naco; even Nogales will be a shock to their systems. You know what it's like, Herb, so why in the world would you wish an assignment like that on a woman like Beth Page?"

His left-handed entreaty had fallen on deaf ears and he set about trying to dissuade Beth the only other way he knew. He asked her to go out with him a week before graduation. To his astonishment, she accepted.

Their training was intensified the last week and Don Genteel, their capable instructor through their twelve-week course, drew up a scenario to demonstrate what might happen to any Patrol officer. It was graphic; it was rough; it was no holds barred as they came down on street criminals. And Beth Page froze. She froze holding an unloaded gun, pointed at a human being; even to save her partner's life, she couldn't pull the trigger.

It shook her badly and even his teasing failed to

bring her out of the depression following her failure to protect her partner—him. She asked him point-blank if he believed women should be in the Patrol and he saw her self-doubt reflected in that question. He gave her his answer and the only date he had with her ended up in a quarrel.

He couldn't give up and as the course drew to a close, he promised her any job she wanted; he cajoled; he threatened—all to no avail. She wouldn't give up. She denied trying to replace Jud Chambers even though admitting she was there because the Patrol was his pride and joy; his life.

"I can help in some way," she told him through clenched teeth one day as he tried to get her to go into administration.

"Any job in Customs will help, Beth. You don't have to be in the Patrol. It's the wrong place for you."

"What job would you give me, Brand?" she asked him quietly. "Receptionist? Radio operator? File clerk?" When he didn't answer, she went on. "Just thank your lucky stars you won't have to put up with me. Perhaps I'll have a tolerant supervisor who thinks I can do the job I'm paid to do."

He didn't tell her he would be anything but a tolerant supervisor, no matter if it did happen to be her he was supervising.

Even a visit to her parents got him nowhere except liking them and tangling his mind up with wanting Beth to be with him and wanting her stationed on the east coast away from the dangers they would face on the southwestern border.

Aside from believing she belonged anywhere but in

the Patrol, he found he was thinking too much about the softness of Beth Page and not enough about the hardships of the job to which they had been assigned. Too much about how it would feel to hold her close and not enough about how she would look if Varro got hold of her.

He spent the days traveling from Georgia to Arizona putting his priorities back in order, making up his mind that Beth was an officer assigned to him and nothing more. The feelings he was beginning to have concerning her were hammered into nonexistence and he could handle them if he kept their relationship as supervisor and employee. He went back to dating Dolores Ayon, one of the secretaries from Customs Headquarters in Nogales, to strengthen his position. They had stopped dating weeks before for some reason he couldn't even remember.

He thought he had managed quite well ignoring Beth except for the time they set her up and, looking at the tiredness in her face, the lingering expression of sadness in the wide gray eyes, he had to kiss her. Her response had brought him back to the reasons he never did that and he pushed her away, leaving a wondering expression on her face.

Last night had almost proved his undoing. If she hadn't gone to sleep early ...

And today they'd be playing hide-and-seek in the desert with known killers; with criminals a slender silvery blond-haired girl meant no more to than the desert squirrels running through the hot sand.

He walked to the bedroom that his parents had used for most of their married life and opened the door.

Moonlight filtered through the sheer curtains that moved with the light breeze coming from the south.

Standing by the bed, he watched her sleep. One hand curled beneath her cheek, the other one lying flat in front of her, long fingers spread open as though bracing herself. And as he watched her the anger returned. *What the hell are you doing here in my house, in my parents' bed, in my outfit where you're apt to...* He stopped his thoughts, reaching down to pull the sheet up over her, and turned away. He was suddenly very, very tired.

Chapter Ten

Beth had no idea where she was. There was little light in the room where she lay in a big four-poster bed, staring up at a beamed ceiling of natural wood. After a long moment of disoriented thoughts, she moved, realizing she wore only panties and bra. Turning her head quickly, she drew a deep breath when she saw the pillow next to her was empty. Her last clear memory was trying to decide who would chaperone whom when they found Luis and Aurelia wouldn't be coming home. Evidently Brand had won that honor.

"Would you like a cup of coffee?" Brand asked from the doorway.

Instinctively, she pulled the sheet up over her and he smiled, walking to the bed, holding a steaming mug. He sat on the edge, waiting for her to take the cup from him.

"G-good morning," she said uncertainly.

"How do you feel?"

She scooted up against the pillow, holding the sheet over her chest, and reached for the coffee. "I feel fine." She glanced around at the barely light room. "What time is it?"

"Six. I hated to wake you, but we'll be leaving here as soon as it gets full daylight."

She nodded, sipping the coffee, remembering the tender kisses they shared the night before; wondering why—always wondering where Brand was concerned.

Aware that he was watching her, she was suddenly shy as she realized again that he had undressed her, not completely, but almost. The skimpy bra and panties left little to the imagination.

His hand moved from his thigh to her leg covered by the sheet, sliding down to reach her foot sticking out from beneath the covers. Rubbing lightly across her instep, he looked around at the foot and bent to kiss her big toe, biting gently into the pink flesh.

At her swiftly indrawn breath, he looked up and smiled. He stood up and moved toward the door. "Breakfast in ten minutes. I'm afraid we have to move."

"Bare toes are sexy," he had once told her.

Left alone, her eyes drifted to her foot, sticking out beneath the bright quilt that covered her. Brand's gentle touch, his kisses last night—what she could remember of them. Was it a turning point for them? Was he going to accept her as his partner and perhaps extend friendlier feelings toward her?

Since they left El Paso, he had gradually withdrawn; he wasn't cold but gave her only a matter-of-fact attention that went with his instructions to his partner. She wasn't sure he regarded her as his partner. It seemed he was biding his time, waiting. Perhaps if they ever ran

into big trouble, he expected her to freeze as she did at
the Academy. Then he would feel obligated to report
her shortcomings in her evaluation that was due at the
end of the quarter.

She swallowed. She had not yet been put to the final
test to see if she could stand up to the rigors required of
Patrol members. Even the first stakeout in Madera Canyon during the threatened nuclear weapons heist hadn't
materialized. Providence could be looking out for her to
give her a chance. Something Brand did not want to do.

This was his territory, she thought, sliding out of bed
to cross to the big windows with a view toward the
south where their surveillance would be. Past the end
of the red-brown mesa, she could see the ragged rise
and fall of the desert terrain with scattered scrub-brush
sage and salt cedar.

Ghost towns, old mines, crevices, and canyons,
Brand said, lots of places for marauders to hide. Yes,
his territory; she was a foreigner.

Dressed, she walked quickly to the kitchen where
Brand was taking up a pan of bacon. A bowl of eggs
followed and he took a pan of biscuits from the oven.

As he looked up, a slight smile touched his mouth,
but not his eyes. "Aurelia always leaves some dough
made up in case I drop in."

"Can I help?"

He nodded. "You can pour our coffees and get the
butter out of the refrigerator."

A moment later they sat down and she drew in an
appreciative breath. "How come you're such a good
cook and never married?"

He didn't answer immediately and she glanced up,

feeling the color sweep into her face. "I'm sorry..." she started to say but he shook his head.

He held the plate of biscuits out to her before he said, "I was engaged once. She married while I was overseas in the marines."

"Oh." She met his eyes for a moment then looked at the biscuits he held, taking one to fill with butter.

"There aren't many eligible women in this area. More men than women. They don't much care for the loneliness and isolation that go with ranching."

Somehow she couldn't picture a woman engaged to Brand who would prefer someone else to him. She frowned at the warm bread she held. Maybe Dolores was accustomed to the isolation and could put up with the loneliness.

She turned her attention to the breakfast, trying to ignore the fact that she was becoming too conscious of Brand's appeal for her. He certainly didn't encourage her.

"We usually start patrols in the evenings," she said into the silence that followed. "Why is this one different?"

"We want to see if there are any tracks or trails that might point to someone being in the area before we make our own paths," he said. "It's not a very well-populated area and tourists seldom find the back trails we'll be on. Once we check it out around Harshaw and Duquesne, if we need to stay out several days, most of it will be evening and night. The only time we'll be off duty is during the hottest part of the day."

Twenty-four hour patrol. "It doesn't get too hot this time of year, does it?"

"Because it's dry, it doesn't seem hot, but yesterday the temperature went to ninety-five degrees."

She really hadn't noticed. The DEA film had effectively wiped everything else from her mind. That film might be replayed if they found the man they were searching for.

Brand checked around and they left, driving the unmarked Customs truck down a narrow dirt and gravel road that wound south from his property.

The area they drove through was monotonously the same. Stretches of flat land with scrubby bushes; soaring mountains that stared back at her with alien glares. *Arizona probably resents my being here as much as Brand does.* Stiffening against the seat, she turned to meet his eyes, hidden as hers were by dark glasses.

They passed a fence with a wooden gate opened all the way back and Brand pointed. "That was the school back in the eighteen-seventies."

A half-wall of adobe crumbled inward over the ruins of the small building. Live oaks grew in what was once the floor. A mile farther, he said, "This was Duquesne at one time. The mines were run by Mexicans before this became the United States."

Back of the sign that said "No Trespassing" was a wooden structure. "That's the entrance to one of the old mines." He let that sink in before he went on. "There are any number of tunnels underneath." That was all he said but she could imagine the rest.

Any number of tunnels for someone on the run to go. It might be dangerous, but it could be a hideout for days without anyone knowing you were there. Anything—or anyone—could be down there.

He drove slowly past the entrance and the road they traveled became little more than a path as they topped a small mountain. He stopped and she drew in her breath at the sight of range after range of mountains stretching into the distance, misty and forbidding, but beautiful.

"This is the Santa Cruz Valley and just over the mountains is Nogales." His voice had gone cold and withdrawn. This was where his friend had been killed. This was where he did not want Beth Page.

"Brand..." She turned as she spoke, but she faced a very different Brand than she had seen last night. He was watching her and she had never seen his eyes so hard, searching deep inside her, searching for the weakness he knew was there.

"Somewhere, those people are waiting for us, Beth. They don't care that you left parents behind you. They don't care that you're in the Patrol out of a misguided sense of loyalty to a man you loved. Remember what Genteel said? They don't care about you. They are looking out for greedy number one."

Staring into the cold gray lakes that were his eyes, she wanted to defend herself but he went on. "It's now, Beth. The time is now. It's too late to think you might freeze with that gun. It's up to you and me, Beth, and you'd better be able to live up to your part of your contract. You'd damn well better NOT freeze."

To Brand, Beth Page was the unwanted burden thrust on him by unthinking superiors and he wanted her to know it in no uncertain terms.

Shock was a part of what she felt. Somehow his gentleness the night before and his thoughtfulness this morning had lulled her into thinking she was making headway toward at least friendship with Brand. He had just set her straight.

Was a misguided sense of loyalty all that had motivated her to join Jud's beloved Patrol? Fingernails cutting into her palms drew her attention to clenched fists lying on her thighs. Slowly letting her fingers uncurl, she rubbed her hands on the legs of her faded jeans, watching the movement almost absently, remembering the decision she had agonized over for six months before submitting her application.

Her gaze lifted to sweep the mountains around them, pinpointing the rugged areas in which the criminals might hide; they might even at that moment be watching them from a well-protected area. Beth's eyes met Brand's uncompromising look, no longer hidden behind dark glasses.

"If I were on the run in a foreign country I wouldn't enter a mine shaft that might cave in on me, where law enforcement personnel would first look for me. Where, if found, the only way out is with someone getting killed, possibly me first," she said slowly and deliberately.

He didn't stir. "What would you do?"

"I'd stay on the border until all the furor died down and special agents were forced to leave for lack of money or purpose."

"What would you do in the meantime if your money is cut off and no more aliens are willing to trust you to take them across?"

"Steal."

He nodded. "And if the agents didn't leave?"

"I'd move along the border on my home turf and

wait for a local crisis or for some of the members of my group to catch up with me."

"Local crisis? Define that."

"Weather." She shrugged. "I don't know. I was just thinking out loud."

The cab of the truck was getting warm and she rolled the window down on her side. A breeze pushed her hair back from her face and she reached in her pocket to bring out the fatigue cap she carried everywhere. With one hand she twisted the heavy hair upward, pinning it with the comb she removed from the back of her head.

He reached with two fingers to capture a strand of hair she missed and tucked it beneath the comb, letting his fingers touch her neck as he withdrew them, leaving a whisper of his touch behind.

She held her breath, but he didn't speak and she pulled the cap down to cover her hair. "Where do we start?" she asked.

"Take the path behind the old mine shaft and work your way northwest from there circling a thousand feet all around. We're looking for anything that might indicate someone has walked through here in the last twelve hours. I'll go south and meet you back here in two hours. The usual signal."

IT WASN'T MUCH. A fuzzy length of black hair caught on the low branch of a skinny water oak at the end of the path that dropped downward over a twenty-foot precipice into a deep wash. Not touching it, she stood looking at the hair and at the drop-off a few yards away. In the past two days, she covered this area at least a dozen times, in the early morning light, in almost total darkness, by faint moonlight. It hadn't been there before, she was certain.

Brand had traded areas with her, had investigated behind her and in front of her. Neither of them had seen any sign of another human being—until now.

Dropping on all fours, Beth moved quickly to the edge, listening as she held her breath. She was about to stand up when the moan came from over the embankment and she hesitated. But only for an instant. She slid forward on her belly, using a clump of buffalo grass to shield her face as she leaned to look down. Movement caught her eye and as she focused on the object at the bottom of the wash, she could only make out olive drab color.

Watching a moment longer, she decided whoever it was wouldn't be going anywhere without help, and slid away to stand up, then she was running in the direction Brand had taken. When she thought she was close enough, she gave the shrill whistle that was their signal, waiting, then again. Not far away, Brand answered.

Back on the path, she lay down again, keeping her eye on the object at the bottom of the ravine, turning often to look in the direction she thought Brand would take to return.

He made no sound as he came almost on the run, dropping beside her as she pointed. She held up one finger to tell him how many people she thought were down there. He nodded.

She sat up and gazed around. Nothing else moved. Brand slipped forward to the bank and leaned down to look.

"Are you injured?" he asked. There was no answer. He repeated the question in Spanish.

A moan was all the sound they heard.

"I'm going down and see how badly he's hurt," Brand said. "Cover me."

She nodded, unfastening her holster and removing the gun, staying just to the side of where Brand had been when he was talking to whoever lay in the wash. As he worked his way through the scrubby grasses on the side of the canyon, Beth pointed the gun at the figure she could now see was a man who was trying to sit up. She didn't see a weapon, but hers was aimed and ready; she watched him without blinking. She would shoot to protect Brand.

Brand, his gun drawn, approached from the side and down a few feet from where the man lay. She couldn't hear what Brand said, but the man shook his head, trying to raise his hands. She saw Brand replace his gun in his holster and still she kept hers trained on them.

"No weapon, Beth. He's hurt and I'll have to drag him up. Keep an eye out around us."

A few minutes later, Brand half carried the injured man up the embankment and put him down in the shelter of the live oak where she had seen the strands of hair.

He was young, he was Mexican, he was terrified and he was half dead.

Brand questioned him, and if he was telling the truth the crew of criminals had retreated to central Mexico to regroup and start over.

"No doubt," Brand said grimly.

"Why did they leave him?" she asked. "He's so young."

"He's lucky they didn't shoot him," he told her tersely, lifting the boy to carry him to the truck. He tied his hands and feet and propped him against the cab in the back.

"They left him enough water and tortillas to last two days and he was trying to find his way to the border when he fell in the gulch."

"Do you believe him?" she asked as they got into the truck and he started back toward his ranch.

"No, but I think he's telling the truth about their being back across the border. You had a pretty good concept of what they'd do yourself, you know."

She didn't answer that but turned to look through the back window of the truck at the young boy. "He doesn't look like a killer."

"He's learning. Don't waste your sympathy on him because he'll be the leader in a couple of years." The grimness of his voice made her shiver. "We'll take him to headquarters and have them call off the stakeout for now. They can hang on to this one for a few weeks; his friends may come back for him.

He drove past the turnoff that led to his house, past the city limits of Patagonia, exceeding the speed limit until he came to Nogales.

"I'll drop you at the office. You can start the paperwork and tell Alfredo I need some fresh coffee."

As the truck pulled away, she stared after it, at the young man in the back, his head dropped to his chest, long black hair blowing across his face.

She looked down at her dirty jeans; at the ripped shirt

she had caught on the spines of a dried cactus. Reaching up, she yanked the fatigue cap off, removing the comb to allow her hair to swing free. Drawing in a deep breath of the dry, clean air, she sent one last look at the truck disappearing down the road.

So much for the capture of her first hardened criminal.

Chapter Eleven

Eventually, the young alien they had picked up on their stakeout recovered from his injuries and was transferred to a detention center for further investigation.

Beth found that normal duties for the Patrol were the boring and long hours of patiently watching and waiting. Informants came forward with information that they diligently checked out, sometimes coming across illegal activities, sometimes coming up with nothing more than skinned knees from crawling around in the desert, routing out more desert squirrels and jackrabbits than anything else.

As the weeks passed, she and Brand became a close team and she was able to guess his next move and what he required of her before he spoke. But as their teamwork got better, he withdrew from any personal attachment to her.

If he looked directly at her it was to issue an order. If he accidentally brushed against her, he pulled away as though it was offensive to touch her. On patrol or stakeout, he kept his distance, no longer giving her even the gentle glances she had encountered a few times and had treasured.

Although it was a pointed rebuff, she was almost glad. No longer did she have to dread his touch and her reaction to it, but a tiny hurt remained, just the same. On the few days they were off the job, he went to his ranch, casually inquiring about her plans and that was all.

One day, he brought her some of Aurelia's jalapeño cornbread and the recipe for it written in his squared-off handwriting.

He stood by the door as she opened the foil-wrapped bread and smelled it, smiling at him as she did so.

"How much leave do you have, Beth?"

"Not many days. I took most of it between school and here. Why?"

"I thought you might want to fly home for a few days. After Christmas, you won't get a chance."

"You've heard something?" she asked, her pulse quickening.

He nodded. "Our friends like to work when they know most people are on holiday, so we'll be on the lookout as they move north. Also another group is stirring on the east coast of Mexico and we aren't sure if they're working their own game or if a rendezvous is planned. If that's the case, we're way outnumbered and could be in big trouble."

"How about reinforcements out of El Paso?" she asked.

"They have their own problems right now, shortage of manpower the biggest of them all."

She looked at the bread in her hands, thinking a

simple pleasure such as this ruined by greedy, destructive human beings who don't bat an eye at murder much less spoiling her appetite. Her gaze lifted to lock with Brand's, seeing her thoughts reflected there.

His lips tightened and he turned to open the door. "Be ready to leave at six tomorrow evening. We'll be out three or four days."

"Yes," she said and listened to his steps on the gravel outside the trailer. She rewrapped the bread and put it on the counter and slowly got ready for bed. As she lay in the quiet darkness, the thought penetrated that she was more than two thousand miles from home in alien territory, in the enemy camp, alone.

It's your own fault, Brand would tell her; I tried to warn you what you were getting into.

All I need is one friend, she wanted to tell him. But she never dared voice that need.

BRAND STOOD at the front window of the office, staring across the few yards to number ten trailer where he had left Beth. Left her because a moment later, he would have had her in his arms, holding her the way he wanted to hold her, helping her relieve the uncertainty inside her.

He couldn't complain about her performance of duties; she was doing an excellent job. The nearest thing to a compliment he had paid her was the recognition of her interpretation of what the men they hunted in the Harshaw area would do if they were smart.

Beth was smart. He smiled. Except where he was concerned. She had not yet recognized the fact that he was having trouble remembering she was a Customs Patrol Officer and his partner. To keep his hands off her when he saw how tired she was; to keep from smiling when she came in from a patrol, dirty and ragged, looking like a little ragamuffin, the heavy ash-colored hair in sweaty ropes when she released it from the funny topknot she kept it in under the old fatigue hat.

I should write Herb and tell him he was right about Beth, but I won't give him the satisfaction, he thought. *He's still wrong about her assignment; she doesn't belong in this place. But, then, who does?*

The lights in the front of Beth's trailer went out and he turned away to pick up a document he had come back to the office to read. After ten minutes of reading the same paragraph without comprehending one word, he put it in the safe, locked the office, and left. Beth's trailer was dark but he stood for a moment watching the windows, glancing around at the moonlit desert surrounding them.

The enemy was known to be moving north and surveillance would start the next night. He'd better get some rest too; it might be a long time before they saw beds again.

As THE HOLIDAY SEASON approached, the weather grew cold and winds swept through the high desert out of the Sierretas and Santa Ritas. On their stakeouts as they waited word on the movement of gun smugglers reported to be heading their way, Beth slept in the cab of the truck while Brand patrolled, swapping every two hours.

Her body grew thin and tight, her legs strong enough that she could bend and crawl with the best of them. Obeying Brand's instructions, she used lotions liberally, keeping her skin soft, and it tanned to a smooth creamy shade, showing off the clear gray eyes, emphasizing the charcoal frame of eyelashes.

Somewhere between Christmas and New Year's Day, she sat on a hillside gazing north across the highest mountains. Snow swept ahead of the winds, a distant sun turning it into a ghostly veil.

Brand came around the back of the truck. "Let's go, Beth."

She moved without asking why or where, hoping it was toward Nogales. She needed a shower in the worst way.

"Do you need to go by home to get a change of clothing?"

"What?" she asked, thinking she had missed part of the conversation.

"We need some time away from this job and I thought a day or two at the ranch would help." He stared straight ahead at the road.

"I have jeans and a flannel shirt," she said.

"That will do," he said and turned the truck toward Patagonia.

They didn't talk. She was puzzled at his attitude and too tired to figure it out. They passed the road that led to hell and a little farther, turned off on the road leading to the small town Brand called home.

Silently, she watched the now familiar landscape glide by letting her thoughts go as they always did to the man beside her. He must be exhausted to give them a couple of days off; she couldn't remember the last time they had two days straight off duty. She was tired, and still she remained intensely aware of Brand. Rubbing her neck with dry hands, she straightened in the seat as she saw they were entering the small town.

The buildings in Patagonia were built in the old western style. What appeared to have once been a railway station now said "Patagonia Municipal Building." They passed the Museum of the Horse and Trading Post where Brand made a right turn toward his ranch. Most trees she had seen in Arizona were scrubby, but the one main street was lined with huge live oaks, fascinating as they stood on the edge of the endless desert.

He parked the truck in the yard back of his house, and she got out to stand stretching. He took their small pouches with their guns from behind the seat and smiled at her.

"A hot shower will help."

She looked around. There were no other cars in the yard and the garage in the back was closed. Since her first visit there, the water oak trees had lost their leaves and bare branches creaked in the wind. The mountains seemed even closer in the clear, brisk air. She took a deep breath and followed Brand into the house.

When he left her in the room she used before, she needed no urging toward the shower and sighed blissfully as the warm water washed away the several days' collection of gritty dust. Her head even felt lighter after shampooing her sticky hair.

After towel drying her hair she dressed and went barefoot through the hall to the kitchen, expecting to meet Aurelia. Instead, she found Brand slicing tomatoes and tending a fluffy omelet. Coffee perked noisily on the counter.

He met her questioning glance. "Aurelia and Luis are in Chihuahua visiting relatives. They usually go over the holidays when things are slow here."

Without asking, she went to the cabinet and took plates and cups to the table. They were hungry and ate in silence. She refilled their coffee cups halfway through the meal.

"Nap time," she said, pushing away her empty plate. Their long hours in the field with sleep broken at regular intervals told on all of them after a while and the warm shower had relaxed her, leaving her groggy.

He nodded. "You deserve it."

She stood up to collect the dishes for the washer, glancing at her watch to see that it was one o'clock. She was being dismissed, took the hint and, in the bedroom, turned the bright quilt back to lie across the bed. It was the last move she remembered for three hours.

REALITY CAME SLOWLY to her as she lay still, looking straight ahead at the solid oak headboard and the thick corner posts of the bed. Her eyes focused on her watch that said it was four o'clock. *It's awfully dark to be four in the afternoon unless I slept all night.* The drapes were drawn and she went to push them aside. The thin December sun had disappeared and dark clouds hovered low, hiding the mountain range to the east.

She went through the house, searching for Brand and had started outside when she saw him astride a huge black gelding galloping toward the corral. Horse and rider seemed made of one piece as he disappeared and a few minutes later, she saw him moving toward the house with long, easy strides.

As he came up on the porch, she pushed the door open. "What happened to your famous southwestern sun?" she asked.

He smiled. "It doesn't want us to get too complacent and occasionally reminds us it's winter. It's New Year's Eve and most people won't mind staying inside a few hours." He pushed the door closed behind him.

"I didn't even remember what day it was," she told him. They never needed a calendar in the field; they moved according to the criminal's timetable.

"Would you like to start celebrating with a margarita?"

"Okay." She thought of the last drink he had made for her when he ended up being chaperone while she slept. Protecting her from what? she wondered idly, watching him as he mixed the drinks at the bar across the room from her. It was a long time since anyone had bothered to make a pass at her.

He had lit a fire in the fireplace and she stood a moment in front of it before she settled against the end of the loveseat and waited for the drink.

"Do you always take your Christmas decorations down before New Year's?"

He came across the room to stop in front of her, handing her a strawberry-tinted drink. "There weren't any put up this year since no one was here to enjoy them." He glanced around. "It is sort of bare, isn't it?" He sat down beside her on the two-cushioned couch.

"Yes," she said, tasting the drink, running the tip of her tongue over her lips. "Mm-m, it's delicious, even if it is cold weather."

"Would you rather go out to eat or cook here?" he asked after a few minutes of comfortable silence.

"Go out where?"

"The Benson Country Club would be the best for dinner. About an hour's drive."

"I don't have anything suitable for a country club," she told him.

He laughed. "Country Club dress code à la Benson is jeans the same as anywhere else out here."

She turned to look at him. "Do you really want me to choose?"

He nodded and his glance dropped to her lips as she licked them. Conscious of a thin trickle of warmth from the tip of her tongue as he watched her, she looked back at the fire.

"Let's make a sandwich and not move from in front of this fireplace close to the bar."

He laughed. "Not a chance. We fix steaks on the grill outside and you have to help."

She shivered. "It's too cold to cook outside."

"The grill is protected from the wind. We'll just grill the steaks and eat indoors. How's that?"

She nodded doubtfully. "A sandwich would be easier."

"Mary Ann would have a fit if she knew I fed you a sandwich on New Year's Eve, Beth. You already look like you've lost weight and she'll think we never feed you."

She grinned. "You gonna cook black-eyed peas?"

"Pinto beans out here," he said. "Come on. Let's get the fire started."

She followed him through the kitchen to the outside on the sheltered side of the house. Near a big oak was a square table with benches on three sides and, nearby, a built-in grill. As he busied himself starting the fire, she sat on one of the benches, watching his movements.

As he bent to work at the fire, she could see the gray in his hair and her thoughts went to Jud. How many times had they done this same thing at Dockery Lake or Lake Lanier? Jud with his laughing eyes, a habit of running his fingers through his sandy hair, of taking her hair to pull it close to her face, saying, "My coordinated Beth, with matching hair and eyes."

His love for her alone—she broke off her thoughts and her nostrils flared as a surge of anger stiffened her body. Anger at his useless death, anger transferred to Brand for not understanding her wish to have some part in what had been Jud's life.

The object of her anger turned to meet accusing wide gray eyes and he straightened away from the blaze that was just starting.

"What's wrong?" he asked, sensing the change in her.

She glanced down at her fingers locked tightly together. "Nothing's wrong." Looking from him to the coals, she said, "You must do this often."

"Enough to keep in practice." He stood opposite her. "Are you sure you're okay? Maybe the drink was too strong."

"No. It's good."

"Let's go look for something to go with our steaks

and you can finish the drink while you make the salad.''

In the Texas-sized kitchen he asked, "Do you like avocados?''

"I'm not too well acquainted with them although we sometimes got them in Florida.''

"Did you go to Florida often?'' he asked.

She was leaning into the refrigerator, searching the crispers. "The winters there are nice," she said. She backed away with two fresh looking avocados, a head of lettuce, and a large tomato. "Do you have lemons?'' she asked as she put her armful on the counter.

"We use limes more than lemons," Brand said.

"Oh, I saw those." She went back to open the refrigerator, but his hand stopped her and she turned into his arms.

He looked straight down into her eyes. "You went to see Chambers often?''

Her breath caught and her eyes widened at the unexpected question. The strength of his hands on her arms kept her from pulling away.

She nodded. "I was there two weeks before he was killed.''

"You could have been in the middle of it," he said, his voice hard.

"Jud had the weekend off and we were on Sanibel Island on the west coast. He wouldn't let me stay in Miami.''

She didn't know what he read in her eyes, but he made a sound deep in his throat and let her go, turning to open the pantry door he was standing near. He took out two baking potatoes and as he looked them over, she turned to get the limes for the salad.

They worked in silence, stepping around each other. He wrapped the potatoes in wax paper, and as she completed the salads she used plastic wrap to cover the dish, then put it back into the refrigerator.

"I'll fix us another drink as soon as I check the coals," Brand said as he went outside.

Beth went to the door to watch as he tested the fire. As he came back toward the house, she moved back to the sink not wanting him to know she had followed his long-legged stride away from her.

"It's about ready. Let's freshen our drinks."

He held out his hand and she took it. He had his glass in his hand and she picked hers up as she passed the table where she had placed it as she fixed the salad.

The blender was in the freezer with the remainder of the drink mix and now she stood close to him as he removed it and set it back on its base, pushing the switch enough to make the drink slush. He poured them and as she took hers from his hand he put his arm around her to lead her to the windows on the west side.

The sun was just dropping behind the fluted white clouds lying across the mountain tops and a gray line lay almost at the peak of the tallest range. An orange-red ball of sun rode the crest and turned the gray layer to gold and silver.

In the silence they watched as the clouds shifted around the sun, changing colors from gold to scarlet and gray. Finally, a mauve drape lifted and the sun disappeared completely behind the black rocks, leaving a rugged outline crested by stars unseen until the brightness disappeared.

She let out her breath and sighed without speaking; there was no need to say anything. She was conscious of Brand's arm around her, his shoulder supporting her head, and she smiled at him in the semidarkness of the room.

Taking his arm from around her, he smiled. "How about that food now?"

"Such mundane things as food after that display but, okay, if you say so."

"Put the potatoes in the microwave and by the time they're finished the steaks will be on our plates." He went outside to take care of the steaks and she put the potatoes in the microwave per his instructions.

She went to the door to call, "Do you have paper plates?"

"No. Use the ones in the cabinet over the sink to your left."

She found the ironstone plates and salad dishes and set the table, using the heavier paper towels for napkins instead of the linen ones in the drawer. *No use to mess up cloth napkins,* she thought.

She heard him coming in and went to open the door, drawing a deep breath of appreciation as he passed her with the still-sizzling steaks.

"Let's see if the smell does them justice," he said and slid her chair forward as she sat down.

They ate like hungry farmhands and when she leaned back and sighed, he asked, "Does it make up for some of the hardtack on surveillance?"

"A little," she admitted. "The drink does the rest."

Together, they cleaned the kitchen and, arm in arm, went back into the living room. He stirred the fire and added a big log as she wandered around, finally stopping by the window where the draperies were still open.

She tingled over her ribs where his big hand had spread over them. She must remember that it was just the moment and the time—a new year coming up. Tomorrow or the next day they'd be polite strangers again.

She leaned over, her forehead against the cool windowpane, straining to see from the light room into the darkness outside.

"Ah, Brand," she said delightedly, "it's snowing. Am I glad we're not out chasing desert squirrels tonight!"

He didn't answer and she turned to find him leaning against the mantel, eyes half closed as he watched her.

"Has your opinion about life in the Patrol changed after three months of boring stakeouts, dodging prairie dogs, chasing desert squirrels, jackrabbits, and mythical marauders?"

She didn't want to answer the casual question. Not because she was trying to be difficult but because she didn't know. During her first six months in Customs, she had formed an opinion, had decided she made the right choice. But that was three months of orientation and three months of school, and no amount of classes really prepared you for what was to come. It conditions you, perhaps, but...

Now after three months on patrol, the uncertainty about being able to perform the duties was gone. Physically and mentally, she had gradually disciplined herself for whatever the Patrol offered. In times of danger a big man presented more of a deterrent to crime, but she offered the element of surprise in her stringent training in self-defense and steamroller tactics.

But she had never really been tested. And no matter

what EEO decreed, prejudice was still alive and kicking in the Patrol. Brand accepted her because he was forced to, not because he wanted to. Not because he didn't think she could do the job but because he thought a man could do it better.

Beth walked slowly toward the fireplace, leaning against the mantel to face Brand. For a long moment, she let her gaze rove over his thin face, the squared jaw that was beginning to show a dark shadow of beard, to his wide mouth that she realized had finally drawn her away from remembering only Jud. True, his purpose was for gentle persuasion to detour her from the Patrol to administration, but he had helped her too whether he meant to or not.

"I don't believe my decision was wrong, Brand. It may not have been the only one that would have worked for me, but I have no regrets." She sipped the drink before she went on. "And what about you? Do you still believe I'm in the wrong outfit?"

"Yes." He answered without hesitation and didn't see her wince as the hard word stuck at the sensitive core of her very being. At least, he didn't mince words; maybe it's better to know where you stand than to dream. She smiled a little.

"Beth," he said but she turned away and went to sit on the loveseat, legs stretched in front of her, staring into the fire.

"Do you have any complaints about my performance?" she asked finally.

"None."

The quiet was interrupted by the breaking of a log on

the fire, shooting sparks behind the screen. Brand put another log on, pulling the broken pieces underneath it so it would burn rapidly.

As he turned Beth yawned, and Brand asked, "Are you going to be awake to see the New Year in?"

"Will it be any different than last year?"

"Not noticeably." He took her glass. "Would you like to try some champagne just in case it is worth celebrating?"

"Champagne?" she asked and at his nod, added, "That sounds like we should be in a ballroom with tux and long flowing gowns of satin and lace."

He laughed and she looked at him to find gray eyes narrowed and filled with lights. It was real laughter and she didn't remember hearing him laugh out loud in a long time.

As they gazed at each other the smile slowly faded from his face, and he turned away to take a bottle from the refrigerator near the bar.

The lights were still in his eyes as he turned to remove the cork from the bottle and she jumped at the loud pop it made. He reached for champagne glasses and poured them half full, turning to hand her one as she walked to meet him.

"To a good year not dominated by chasing desert squirrels," he toasted as their glasses touched.

"Amen." Her voice was fervent and his eyes darkened as she looked up at him. She sipped the bubbly liquid still looking up at him.

Slowly, he took the glass from her, placing them both on the mantel, turning to pull her close to him. He laced his hands behind her neck, fingers going into her hair, pulling her head gently upward until she was on her toes, leaning into his body. His lips touched hers lightly, lingering until hers parted, letting him inside the warm moist opening where he explored thoroughly with the tip of his tongue until she moaned, trying to pull away.

Her body felt weightless, feathery wings lifting her as he brushed her mouth, turning his head side to side, letting his teeth graze as he feasted on the softness of her.

"Please?"

"Beth," he whispered. "Honey." One hand left her head to slide over her shoulder, swiftly down to spread over the small of her back, keeping her close to feel the hardening of his body. Her protests faded as he found her lips again, using both hands to keep her molded to him.

Unable to bend away from him, she went limp in his arms, her fingers digging into his shoulders. Murmuring softly, he moved to her ear, his breath warming the inner rim, his tongue roughly caressing.

She sucked in her breath only to find his mouth over hers again, claiming that breath before it became hers, taking possession of her breathing, her heartbeat, her mind. Her eyes opened wide but the illumination inside of her flashed and the charcoal lashes settled against her cheeks; the dancing shadows trembling through her merged and became heated pinpoints welding them together.

"Oh, honey," he whispered. "You're so sweet, Beth." He buried his face in her throat while his hands sought every part of her body outlined in the tight jeans.

She tried to draw away, swallowing over the hammering in her throat. "How—how can you bawl me out so often and then—then—do this?" She stammered like a sixteen-year-old.

His lashes lifted and he searched her face, meeting her questioning gray gaze. "I bawl you out to keep from doing this."

Lips moving lightly, Brand covered her face, hesitating once more over her parted lips. "Do you understand, darling?"

"No. No, I don't know what you're talking about. You always criti—"

His arms slid down her body and he lifted her, bending his head to keep his mouth on hers as he strode from the room, down the hall to the bedroom. With a quick move, he turned the quilt back and placed her on the bed. Her shirt had come unbuttoned and he pushed the lacy cups of her bra upward, supporting her small breasts with his hands. The dark nipples grew rigid beneath his thumbs as he drew circles around them.

His breath was warm on the dark crests and he lifted his head to look down at her, her breath ragged and deep in her chest as he kissed her, holding the kiss as he unzipped her jeans to allow his hands to go under her panties to stroke her flat belly.

"Brand." She twisted away but he lay beside her, holding her to trail warm kisses on her throat, downward to pull the taut bronze tip into his mouth, wrapping it with his tongue.

"Oh," she whispered softly and stopped struggling to hold him to her. The universe swung in rainbow colors, turning her slim body into liquid fire, surging upward to melt into Brand's hardness.

He lifted his head, smiling into wide eyes, and pulled the jeans and panties off, putting his hand on her shoulder to let his fingertips pursue each curve of her body down to her thighs. He spread his fingers across her, watching as her lips parted and a look of panic touched her expression.

"No." She shook her head, twisting. "No, not here. You..."

He brushed his lips across hers. "No one has slept here but you since my parents, Beth. No one." Gazing into her wide eyes for a moment longer, he whispered, "You don't know how much I've wanted to hold you like this. You can't know..." He groaned as his hands moved over her body.

She lay quietly then as he finished undressing her, taking his time to kiss and caress and smile at her when her body trembled. He bent to kiss her belly, the tip of his tongue outlining her ribs as he went upward to the swell of her breast.

The path he explored was painfully sweet and she drew in a sharp breath as her body shook with her response. He released the soft breast from the warm moistness to gaze down at her as his hand lingered in the warmth of her thighs and she turned to imprison his hand between her legs.

She unfastened his belt, fumbling with the zipper until he stretched, moving his legs to help her. Their clothing discarded, they lay close, touching, feeling the contours of each other's bodies. He took her hand from his chest, guiding it down across him.

When she resisted, he whispered, "Yes," and kissed her. "Yes, sweetheart."

Still she hesitated, putting her head back on the pillow to see him better. Her eyes widened as her hand explored and he moaned softly, closing his eyes tightly as she continued to search and caress.

When he could endure it no longer, he turned her on her back and without urging from him she moved to help him. Her tight muscles refused to give for an instant and he hesitated until she brought her legs around him, lifting her hips to meet the thrust of his body.

She gasped and he kissed her, freeing her mouth reluctantly so they could breathe, and only Brand heard her cry out as together they reached heights neither had reached before.

The thundering of two heartbeats quieted as he held her. "Now do you understand, Beth?" he asked against her slightly damp hair.

"Yes, I think so." She kissed his throat and bit gently into the skin. "Yes," she repeated and his arms tightened.

Lying in his arms, she didn't think at all, remembering only what had just happened. Her body tingled where it touched his and she moved her head on his shoulder to see if he was as entranced as she.

His eyes were closed and she thought he had gone to sleep. She touched his lips lightly with one fingertip, a firmly molded mouth that brought all her feelings to the surface, feelings she had buried months ago;

turned her into a desiring female, wanting to give all of her to him; wanting all of him for herself.

Brand's lashes lifted and she was staring into eyes dark with wanting her. He turned on his back pulling her on top of him and she lowered her face to his. His lips parted to accept her kiss, drawing her tongue inside to play with her. Her body straightened as his hands cupped her buttocks and she brought her legs up so that she was half kneeling over him. He pulled her hips down, arching his back to enter her and both of them moaned as he succeeded. In her position she couldn't move, but he began a slow up and down motion, easier for him now than it had been the first time.

"Kiss me, Beth," he said and she bent to him again. One hand left her hips to bring her head closer and his kiss was hard and demanding, his tongue thrusting inside her mouth the same as his body, forcing itself with rhythmic movements into hers.

There was no ocean, but waves lifted them, held them in a lovers' swell of softness, floating with the tide until it peaked too intensely to endure.

"Darling!" he cried out with his heated release into her and she sighed, slowly relaxing in his tight embrace.

He turned, letting her body slide off him to rest her head on his arm, but he didn't let her go. He stroked her with gentle sweeps of his fingers, over the hip resting against his, spreading his big hand over her curving firmness.

"Happy New Year, darling," he said.

Her cheek resting on the roughness of his chest, one hand beneath his arm on his ribs, she answered,

"Yes," and went to sleep, a smile curving her lips.

"YOU TRY NOT TO FOLLOW any set pattern, don't you?" the voice accused her gently.

She opened her eyes to look straight into Brand's, inches from her on the same pillow. A shadow of beard darkened his skin and she moved her hand from around him to rub his bristly chin. On her way across his face, her fingers touched lips that parted as he too recalled their lovemaking.

"Pattern?" she repeated as he kissed her fingers.

"Women are supposed to look frightful when they wake up. Makeup smeared, hair a mess." He used one hand to brush her tumbled hair back from her cheek, curving his fingers around her throat. His eyes grew darker as he studied her face from the charcoal fringe of lashes around the light gray eyes, down the pert nose to pale, rose-colored lips.

"Oh, Beth." He pulled her to him and they lay close, not talking.

The room was in semidarkness and she could only guess at the time, but time didn't matter. Eyes closed, lips parted against his throat, she remembered the night of love, aware they had done the wrong thing for two people in their position. Brand's animosity disappeared for the night in their coming together as lovers, in the need to forget what might happen to them tomorrow.

What would be their reaction to each other now every time they touched, every time their eyes met? Would he mark last night down as a conquest not to be acknowledged in the light of day? Such a relationship couldn't be ignored, could it? Not by her—she would never forget. But Brand?

His arms tightened and he brought her naked body into the shape of his. His hard body pressed into her flat belly and she drew in a sharp breath, conscious of her answering desire for him.

"I need a shower," she whispered.

"Now?" he protested, his hands exploring the softness curved against him.

"Yes, now," she insisted.

He held her a moment longer and sighed. "You're an odd creature, Beth," he said.

"I don't fit the mold of your other girls, Brand?" she asked, then held her breath because she hadn't meant to say anything like that, had not intended to mention any other girls. She really didn't want to know about Dolores or the girl who married while he was overseas.

He caressed her cheek, running his fingers over her lips, pushing her hair behind her ear and outlining the lobe, coming downward to touch the pulse beating wildly in her throat.

"I don't remember any other girls."

He turned the cover back and slid from the bed, looking over her slim body before he bent to lift her. He kissed her hard on the mouth and strode into the bathroom with her, standing her on the carpeted floor. He reached to turn on the shower, holding her with one arm as he adjusted the water temperature.

"Do you want the heat turned up?" he asked.

"I'm not cold," she said, smiling up at him.

"Come on," he said.

She held back. "Both of us?"

His eyebrows lifted. "Aren't you interested in con-
servation, Beth? Arizona has a shortage of water."

She stared at him and let her glance go down the
hard-muscled body of the man holding on to her arm.
From wide shoulders to narrow hips, to hard thighs and
back to meet the amusement in his eyes, she looked
him over.

"You have beautiful legs," she said.

He pulled her into the marble-lined shower with
him. "So do you, among other things." He turned her
around, facing away from him. "Do you want your hair
wet?"

"No. I should have pinned it up."

"I'll be careful." His voice was ragged over the
sound of running water as he put his hands on her hips
and moved closer to her.

She closed her eyes, letting the water spray them,
conscious of his hard body pressing into her. He had a
bar of soap in his hand and began to lather her body,
beginning at her breasts, leaving them soapy, the
nipples strutted outward as he worked downward. He
reached her thighs, placed the soap in the dish, and
used both hands to rub over the mass of dark blond
hair. She whimpered a little as his fingers explored inside her and she leaned against him as her legs became
weak.

"Honey," he whispered, turning her around to face
him.

The water hit her shoulders and splashed into his
face but neither noticed. He stared into her wide open
eyes for only an instant before his mouth found hers,
wet and cool, and he kissed hard. At the same time, he

stooped, guiding himself into her slippery body. It became harder to breathe and he was forced to stop kissing her, their bodies straining to get closer to each other.

"Oh," she whispered. "Oh." She held on to him as he moved in long, slow motions and, suddenly, she gave a soft husky sound, almost a scream, her eyes wide open looking into his as he, too, cried out, holding himself deep inside her until release for both of them was complete.

Water ran over them as they leaned against the wall, still together. As he withdrew from her, she trembled and held on tightly as he caught her to him for a moment, then turned her around to begin bathing her again. When he finished, he turned off the water, rubbed her dry with a towel and wrapped another one around her.

"Your hair's wet, Beth," he said.

Dreamy eyes stared into his. "It doesn't matter."

He smiled and kissed the softly parted lips. "Go wrap up and keep warm." He pushed her toward the door.

She did as she was told and a few moments later, he came from the bathroom, a towel wrapped around his hips. He sat on the bed.

"Well it's another year. Do you feel older than you did last year?"

"I feel quite young," Beth said and a blush spread over her face.

He laughed. "You even act young. I must admit it's the kind of youth I enjoy." He touched her cheek. "I'll dress and put on some coffee. I might even bring you a cup to have in bed." His eyes went the length of her body outlined beneath the covers. "And I could join you."

"I'll get up and dress."

"Killjoy," he said. He patted her hip and went out of the room, down the hall to his bedroom and she heard a door close.

She lay back on the pillow she had shared with Brand and let her hand slide over the hand-embroidered pillow slip where his head had rested beside hers. Her body, wrapped only in the thick towel, was alive and glowing and an ecstatic shiver shook her as she recalled the end of the old year and the beginning of the new.

What did the new year hold in store for them? What kind of relationship would they have to withstand the hardships in the Patrol? Would he allow his feelings to show in their everyday job? How could they deny the desire that kindled and exploded, bringing a warm satisfaction to her slim body?

Still musing on these questions, she dressed in jeans and a yellow plaid flannel shirt, toweled her hair until it was just damp, and went to the kitchen in search of Brand. He was pouring coffee into two mugs.

"I lit the fire in the living room. Let's go in there."

She preceded him into the room and walked to the window. It was gray outside, the clouds hovering close, and occasionally a flake of snow whirled ahead of the wind. The light snow that had started about midnight had not amounted to much and had been blown away except for a few protected spots.

"Did you hear a forecast of the weather?" she asked.

"No. It doesn't matter to us until tomorrow," he

said, close by her shoulder. She leaned against him and
his hand came around to rest on the front of her jeans,
fingers idly tracing the zipped fly. They stayed that way
until his thighs, resting against her hips, moved and
she turned in his arms to look up at him.

"How could you?" she asked, pressing her slimness
into him.

"It's easy," he said, smiling. "Interested?"

With her head tilted to watch him, she appeared to
consider the question. The dark gray of his eyes held an
unfamiliar tenderness that intrigued her and she stood
on tiptoe to put her lips lightly to his.

"Yes, but can we wait a little while? My hair's still
wet."

Sighing, he turned her back toward the couch. "If
you say so, Beth, but speaking of hair, I'll be right
back."

She sat on the couch, staring into the golden flames
of the fire until she heard his footsteps coming back
and she raised her head to smile at him. He carried a
small package, wrapped in rose-sprigged paper and tied
with a rose-and-white-striped ribbon.

He handed it to her and at the question in her eyes
said, "It was for Christmas, but I didn't have a chance
to give it to you."

"For Christmas?" she said slowly. "Why would you
buy me a Christmas present, Brand? Isn't it against
regulations or something?"

"Probably," he said and grinned. "But I promise not
to tell if you don't. Open it."

Hesitantly, she slipped the ribbon off, broke the tape
holding the sides, and removed the paper, running her

fingers over the black suede of the elongated case. She touched the small clasp at the front and the lid opened upward and her breath caught at sight of the curved combs lying inside. Dark gray with a lighter mother-of-pearl inlay along the base, it was a striking pair. She took out one of them, running her fingers over the smooth decoration and down the wide teeth that would hold well in her thick hair.

"They're lovely, Brand," she said, looking at him as he sat beside her. "I'll be afraid to wear them."

"Wear them, Beth. You won't lose them if they're fastened in that mop of hair." His hand tangled in the subject of their conversation, pulling her head back to place his mouth on hers. Her hands clasped behind his head and her lips moved beneath his warm demanding mouth.

Her hands rested on his thighs for a moment then moved slowly toward his body, fingers pressing into his hard flesh. His breath quickened and he slipped one hand beneath her to lift her hips, pulling her onto his lap.

"Your hair's dry, honey." His whispered words were husky.

Feathery lashes lifted slowly to meet his gaze and her hands moved to frame his face. Her thumbs caressed his lower lip. "Brand."

She buried her face in his shoulder as he lifted her to walk slowly to the bedroom, kissing her lightly as he placed her on the bed. He concentrated on removing her clothing and when he had finished, stood looking down at her before he undressed and lay beside her.

Without urging from him, she turned on her side to

face him, stroking his skin with light fingers until he shivered and pulled her into his arms.

"I can't wait, darling," he said and took her with slow, easy movements. She responded, stretching her legs outward and bringing them over his narrow hips, holding him deep within her. It couldn't last. He called her name in the moment of spellbinding blaze of glorious satiation.

"A wonderful way to die," she breathed into his kiss.

"Yes, my darling, yes." He held her, breathing in the scent of their love.

Chapter Twelve

He held her a long time and as they lay close, she drifted into a light doze, breathing evenly.

"Beth?"

"Mm-m," she answered, half asleep, sliding her hand over his hip.

"Stop it," he ordered.

"All right," she said and put her arm across his ribs.

"Would you like to call Jim and Mary Ann?"

She put her head back on the pillow to look at him. "From here?"

"You don't have to tell them you're in bed with me, do you?"

"No, but..." She hesitated.

"Just dial, honey. They won't know you aren't at home."

"I know, but it costs a lot to call to the East Coast," she reminded him.

"I'll work some overtime to pay it for you," he promised. "Now, go call your parents while I fix breakfast."

"I'm glad you finally recognized equal rights for women," she said, her voice smug.

"Are you hungry?" he demanded, fixing her with a stern gaze.

"Yes," she replied in a meek voice.

"Then watch your tongue," he advised, going out the door.

She grinned at his back and dressed, following him to the kitchen.

"There's a phone in the living room," he said as he looked up to see her standing in the doorway.

"I wanted to make sure you were still here," she said, her eyes full of faraway thoughts.

"I'll be here, Beth," he assured her.

She wet her lips, hesitating, before turning toward the living room. Once she had thought Jud would always be there. She picked up the phone and dialed and was surprised the call went straight through. Maybe it was early yet for most New Year celebrators to be up making phone calls. It was ten o'clock eastern time.

"Page residence," Mary Ann said in her soft drawl.

"Happy New Year, Mother."

"Beth, honey, we've been trying to call you but no answer. Happy New Year."

Beth crossed her fingers, smiling as she said, "We haven't been out of the desert long, Mother. Thanks for the package. I almost didn't get any of the cookies before they were all gone."

Jim came on the line from another room. "Hi, Beth, honey. How's the job? Any problems?"

"Not really, Dad." She wanted to tell him she had had two days of great relationship with her supervisor and thought Jim would most likely even be happy about that. "You should see me; I look like a gray-haired Indian." She turned as Brand's arms went around her waist and her breath caught at the look in his eyes.

With further assurances that she was fine and would write, she replaced the receiver and turned into his arms. He kissed her lightly from her forehead to her chin and raised his head.

"Gray-haired Indian?" He looked at her hair and into almost matching eyes. "It's pure silver and worth it's weight in gold."

She widened her eyes. "That's from Thoreau, isn't it?"

He grinned. "I wouldn't know. You're the teacher." He led her back to the kitchen. "Breakfast awaits, your womanship."

He waited till she sat down and slipped the chair up to the table before he sat opposite her.

"How are Jim and Mary Ann?"

"Great. They tried out the new van around Thanksgiving up on Baldy Mountain. Almost froze to death according to Mother." She spread butter on a piece of toast. "They miss me."

He reached out to touch her arm. "I know. You have a year in the service, Beth, but you can still resign if you want to."

She met his look silently, trying to gauge his feelings after the past eight hours. She put down her fork. "You want me to leave and go back to language instruction, Brand?"

He didn't look away. Instead, his mouth hardened as

he answered her. "Things are not going to get better, Beth. The DEA briefings tell us that the buildup is gaining momentum. The buildup for every criminal activity ever known to the east and gulf coasts and our southwestern border. It can take any form, Beth, from the simplest smuggling job to the bloodiest type of terrorism and we are going to be in it up to our eyebrows."

"And you want me to run?"

"Oh, God, honey..."

"Did you think making love to me would change my mind?" she asked softly. "Is that what you wanted, Brand?" She continued to watch him as the expressions on his face flitted in quick changes. "For once, your plans backfired, Brand. Nothing would make me leave you now. Nothing. Is that clear?"

They stared at each other and the tenderness in his eyes was there for her to see. He leaned over and took her chin in his hand.

"Why, Beth? Why won't you leave me?" he asked, smiling into her eyes.

The shrill sound of the telephone kept her from answering him, but he let it ring three times before he released her chin and moved to answer it.

He spoke into the mouthpiece, still watching her, then his eyes narrowed and he turned his back, listening for a long time.

Trying not to hear, she cleaned the table and put dishes in the washer, straightening things on the counter. She couldn't leave all their clutter for Aurelia to face when she got home.

"Tomorrow?" he asked. "When does it look like the

action will be?'' He listened again, turning around to face her. His face looked drawn and never had she seen such a hard expression. He nodded twice and said, ''Okay,'' hanging up the receiver.

On a swiftly indrawn breath, he straightened, shoving his hands into the back pockets of his jeans. Her heart jerked at the tight, drawn lines on his face.

His voice was quiet when he finally spoke. ''We'd better get ready to leave, Beth. I have to be in El Paso for a meeting tomorrow.'' His smile was weary and did not reach the gray of his eyes to light them. ''It's too late for you to run.''

Her throat went dry. ''They know when?''

He nodded and walked to her, putting his hands on her arms. ''No matter how you interpret my meaning, Beth, I wish you were in Dahlonega.''

''I want to be with you,'' she said.

He kissed her hard on the mouth. ''Get your things together and I'll lock up.''

She stood by the steps until he pulled the unmarked Customs truck around to her and climbed in beside him. He took one last look around before he pulled from the yard. He didn't speak, and ignoring the seat belt she slid across to sit close enough to touch him.

They rode in silence until they reached the road that turned right by the airport. She stiffened and when he still didn't speak moved to the side of the seat and fastened the belt.

''I need to know that it really happened,'' she said, her slow voice making her drawl more pronounced. He didn't answer for so long that she turned sharply, eyes wide and frightened. The truck swerved to the shoulder of the road and he stared straight ahead for a moment before he turned to her.

"I wish it hadn't happened yet, Beth. God knows I fought long enough to keep it from happening. You should have listened to me, honey." He swore under his breath, reaching for her. "Sweetheart." His mouth covered hers, hard and possessive an instant, going tender and warm before he let her go.

He smiled down at her, his eyes hidden now by stubby lashes. "Did I ever tell you that you have the cutest southern drawl?"

He took his arms away and pulled the truck back onto the highway. She sat still, going over his words. "What were you fighting, Brand?" she asked finally.

He snorted. "What the hell do you think I was fighting, Beth? You. I was fighting you and what you were doing to me."

She couldn't answer, staring dumbfounded at him. He had kept his fight private for she had never suspected anything. When he turned to look at her, his expression softened.

"I wish it hadn't happened yet for another reason, Beth. I wish we still had it to discover, to find out what it is to possess you after wanting you for so long. What it's like to give myself to you. I want it all over again, Beth."

His hands clenched around the steering wheel. "We've worked with false alarms, boring patrols, and fruitless stakeouts, but there's no doubt that there has been a move of gigantic proportions from central Mexico. The Coast Guard, Drug Enforcement, and Customs Patrol are closing in on the activity along the Gulf Coast from Florida to East Texas. They have reason to believe that members of several gangs involved in kidnapping, bootlegging of electronics technology and high-powered weapons split away from a group infiltrating upward through the central United States and are heading this way."

He turned the truck onto Mariposa Road and a few minutes later into the gravel yard at the office. He turned to take in her pale face lifted toward him.

"I have to be at the meetings at headquarters here tonight and leave early tomorrow for El Paso to attend the briefings there. I won't know much more than that until I get back."

Stiffly, they got out of the truck and removed their things to take into the office where Alfredo was waiting for them.

"Happy New Year, Alfredo," she smiled and he grinned.

"Short vacation, yes?"

"Nonexistent, Alfredo. Any more details?" Brand's mouth was a straight line.

"No. They have some messages at headquarters and some are at DEA."

"Did you get in touch with Ward and Milt?"

"Yes. They're ready to move and were going to touch base with the special agents out of Yuma." He held up an envelope. "The messenger picked up your tickets this morning. You leave at five tomorrow morning."

Brand took the envelope. "The way things are moving, we'll be in the desert within three days, Beth. Get some rest and look over the operations schedule on my desk while I'm gone."

She nodded, feeling a heavy weight in her chest. She

cleaned her gun, gave it to Alfredo to lock up, collected her mail and went to number ten, giving only a brief glance at the gray clouds overhead.

Her moves were automatic as she turned the heat up and separated her laundry. She placed it near the door and put coffee on to make, picking up her mail to look through while she waited. There was a Christmas card with a letter enclosed from Smitty.

She smiled as she read:

"I finally convinced Ted I'm the perfect mate for him and we've set the date for June 15. You will be a bridesmaid, won't you? Save your leave so the 'judge' can't deny your request. By the way, do I detect a note of regret that Brand Page is unreachable? Something brewing between you and your so-quiet partner?"

Putting the letter down, she went for a cup to pour steaming coffee into it. From the stool where she sat, she stared through the big window at the front of the trailer. It was filmed with blowing dust so the world outside looked hazy.

Something brewing between you and your so-quiet partner? How perceptive of Smitty and how careless of me. No longer brewing, it was a fully developed storm of emotion for her and she had no idea what it was to Brand.

"I wish we still had it to discover," he had said. "To possess you . . ."

The knock startled her. The knob turned, but Brand's constant reminders and threats had worked and she automatically locked a door when she went through it. She set her cup on the counter and started across the floor.

"Beth?" Brand said quietly.

She slid the lock back and opened the door, unhooking the storm door in one movement. He came inside, pushing the door closed behind him and stood looking at her.

"I'll probably call you from El Paso Sunday, Beth," he said. "The meetings will go on through Monday and I should be home Monday night. I'll know more about the job then, hopefully."

"I didn't think the federal government worked weekends, especially holiday weekends." She smiled a little. "Except Customs Patrol, of course."

"Our friends are counting on that, I'm sure, so when they hit our area, maybe we'll have a surprise for them." He came toward her where she had retreated to the stool, and when he held out his arms, she went into them. He held her tight, finally pushing her away.

"I'll be at headquarters until all hours tonight, Beth, and I won't see you before I leave tomorrow."

"How will you get to the airport?"

"Alfredo will take me." He tipped her chin and kissed her, murmuring against her mouth and she answered him as he probed with the tip of his tongue.

Abruptly, he pushed her away. "You wouldn't want me to miss this briefing, would you?" He touched her cheek and went to the door. "Be sure to study the OPLAN carefully, Beth."

He was gone, leaving her frightened and resentful. Frightened for what they might have to face soon and resentful that he left her here to study dull operations plans while he got all the exciting news. She shivered, admitting to herself that she wasn't interested in going to the meetings to hear the exciting news.

Unplugging the coffeepot, she walked up the gravel driveway to the office. "Where is the OPLAN Brand wanted me to study, Alfredo?"

"On his desk back there. It's the one with the 'secret' cover, so give it to me when you finish."

"Okay." The only furniture in the room that served as Brand's office was a small metal desk, two straight chairs, and two file cabinets. A plastic pencil holder, a two by three inch memo pad, and the secret document were the only items on the desk. She picked up the heavy book and went back into the room with Alfredo, dropping into the chair at the desk near the front of the window.

"Want a cup of coffee to keep you awake?" Alfredo asked.

She smiled at him. "You mean this isn't terribly exciting?"

"Rather dull as a matter of fact," he said, placing a cup of coffee near her.

She gave an exaggerated sigh. "I was told the Patrol was fraught with danger and excitement."

"Not in that book," he told her, going back to the paper he was typing.

Sipping on the coffee, she went through the narrative and diagrams of the plans, fighting to keep her eyes open. As she came to the last page, she saw added instructions in Brand's familiar handwriting: "See attached memo."

She grunted in disgust and stood up, slapping the cover closed. "If they'd write this stuff in plain English instead of mumble-ese, we'd know what we're supposed to do. I read all that and now I have to read a memo to explain it. Who explains the memo?"

Alfredo laughed. "You've been Brand's partner so long, you sound just like him. He's forever calling headquarters and asking 'What the hell do you mean, see reference a to reference c and d? Tell me what you want done and I'll do it.'"

Startled, Beth looked at Alfredo and back at the book. Slowly, she turned to the page that said "See attached memo" and flipped it over to see a brief handwritten note in the form of a memo of instruction.

TO: Beth   1 January
FROM: Brand
SUBJECT: Project initiated New Year's Day
1. Plans never to marry superseded by the following:
   a. I love you.
   b. Will you marry me?
2. Verbal reply required no later than 4 January.

Swallowing over the lump in her throat, she read and reread the memo, removing the page from the back of the classified plan and folding it to put into her pocket.

"Still don't understand it?" Alfredo asked sympathetically. "Brand's good at interpreting those complicated plans and he'll be back long enough before you hit the surveillance to help you figure it out."

"I'm sure I'll have some questions for him," she

said as she passed him the plan. "Thanks for the coffee. See you tomorrow."

Beth rinsed her cup and hung it on the hook by the sink and walked out into the darkness lit only by the dim bulb that burned all the time outside the office. She let herself into her own place and stood looking straight ahead at the lamp she had left on so she wouldn't have to return in the dark.

Her watch said eight o'clock. Twelve hours ago, straight out of Brand's arms, she had talked to her parents. Thirty minutes later, her New Year's fantasy world crashed around her with the shrill ring of the telephone.

Why hadn't he said he loved her this morning? Why did he leave, not saying anything except "read the OPLAN"? He wished she was in Georgia, even admitting it straight out, without softening the sting of it. Now he made her throw out all her beliefs and thinking and start over with his memo of love to her.

Will the real Brandon Page please stand up?

She began to shiver and got up to walk the length of the small room, back and forth, rubbing her hands on her arms.

The phone rang and she stopped pacing to stare at it. Eight forty-five. Alfredo was probably getting ready to leave the office, she thought, as she picked up the receiver, shaking her head to clear her mind of the confusing questions that kept coming at her,

"Page," she said into the receiver.

"Beth, honey, I only have a few minutes' break," Brand said. "Did you finish reading the plan I told you to study?"

"Y-yes."

He waited and when she didn't say any more, he said, "And the memo, Beth?" His voice was softer than she had ever heard it.

Her own voice was a mere whisper. "Yes, Brand." She cleared her throat. "I don't understand."

She detected a smile in his voice as he said, "I thought it was one of the most straightforward memos in the history of the Treasury Department."

"Yes, but you—" She broke off and started over. "Yes, but—Oh, Brand, help me."

"How do you feel about me, Beth?"

"What—what do you mean?"

"Do you love me, is what I mean, honey. Tell me."

It came out in a rush. "I love you very much, but I thought you didn't want me in your outfit."

"You're mixing everything, honey. My not wanting you in the Patrol has nothing to do with my loving you. Nothing," he repeated.

There was an interruption and he said, "I have to go, Beth. I'll call you from El Paso as soon as I get a chance, no later than Monday morning, I'm sure."

She was left with the dial tone buzzing in her ear and slowly replaced the receiver.

Her preparations for bed were automatic as she ran the events of the past few days over in her mind. On the stakeout it had been the same as all their others—brief, impersonal exchanges having to do with the areas they covered and changing from lookout to rest period. When he took her to his ranch, it started out as a routine visit until they talked about the New Year and opened the champagne.

Her body came alive as she recalled Brand's every word and touch, but even though they made love—oh, yes, the sweetest love!—he hadn't mentioned loving her. Had he thought of Jud and wondered about her memories? They were bittersweet memories and the hurt was there.

But it's a different hurt and I can love Brand without losing Jud's memory, she thought. *I'm not required to forget him completely; not ever, but he wouldn't want to interfere with my happiness. Jud was not that kind of person.*

What about the girl Brand had planned to marry? "I don't remember any other girls," he had said. He would have to accept her memories of Jud as she did his memories.

Did he want her out of the Patrol even now? Would he send her back to Georgia? She remembered Brand's warning: The worst confrontations were yet to come.

Saturday and Sunday were unending as she waited word from Brand. She did her laundry and ran; she painted her toenails a bright red and put colorless polish on her short fingernails. In desperation she took out her copy of *The Spy Who Loved Me.* Maybe they'd be luckier than Fleming's spy, she hoped. She left a book of poems by Keats on her bed, but she didn't open it.

Unable to be still, she paced the floor Sunday night, wishing Alfredo would come to the office for some reason—any reason. The phone rang and she answered impatiently. "Page here."

"Hello, Beth." She sucked in her breath at the sound of Brand's voice.

"Brand. Oh, I'm so glad you called."

His question came quickly. "Is something wrong?"

"No. No. I mean—" She bit her lip and waited.

"Sweetheart, listen. I'll be in tomorrow at three. The move has been more rapid than they thought and we pull out by six. I'll call Alfredo early in the morning and he has the orders. Read them carefully."

Her hand on the phone hurt as she gripped harder.

"Beth?"

"Yes, Brand." She was surprised at the evenness of her tone. "Yes. I'm listening."

"Did you think about the memo?"

"Yes," she said, closing her eyes tightly.

"And?" he questioned. "Will you marry me, Beth?"

"Y-yes."

"You don't sound too sure," he said, teasing her.

She was cross and her head hurt from trying to figure him out. "I'm *not* sure, Brand. I'm not sure at all about what's going on."

He laughed softly. "I'll fill you in when I get home. Get plenty of rest tomorrow, Beth. I love you."

He asked me to marry him and I said yes, she thought, surprise tightening her body as she sat there, her hand still resting on the phone. *What will Smitty say to that?* She laughed aloud. *I don't even know what to say. What will Dad and Mother think?* She thought wistfully of calling them but she had talked to them on Friday and they would think something was really wrong.

I need to clarify my own feelings before I explain to them, she decided.

BRAND KNOCKED on her door at four thirty Monday afternoon and she was in his arms before the door clicked shut behind him. He held her close, neither of them speaking.

He pushed her slightly away to look into her face. "Tell me, Beth."

"I love you, Brand, and I'll marry you." She was smothered against his chest for an instant. "How long have you known you loved me?" she demanded.

He sighed. "Don't ask, honey. It's been a long, uphill battle to keep you out of my arms."

"Kiss me," she said, standing on tiptoe, and his mouth was gentle as it covered hers, but she couldn't leave it that way. There was a lot of time to make up for and they would soon be on a stakeout where all their attention would be given to staying alive.

Her parted lips allowed her tongue to seek inside his mouth against his teeth. He moaned softly before he lifted his head, breathing hard. He pulled her head to his shoulder, fingers working into her thick hair.

"We have to go, Beth. I have calls to make and a report to write for headquarters." He pulled her head back to look down at her. "Be more careful than ever, darling. This is the real thing; we aren't playacting and neither are the ones we'll meet. I'll tell you more as we go out, but right now, Beth, you do understand this is the one we've been waiting for all these months."

"Yes, I understand."

He stared down into her upturned face. "I wish there was time to get you some leave papers and send you home." He shook his head and smiled. "Still, I can't think of anyone I'd rather have with me."

"Do you trust me now, Brand?"

"With everything I have."

She didn't speak but held onto him. *Nothing is going to happen to us,* she vowed. *Nothing. We have our whole lives together ahead of us.*

"Sweet, sweet," he whispered and reluctantly let her go. "I have things to do, Beth. Meet me at the office in thirty minutes."

She stood in the door watching his slim figure swing across the gravel separating the trailers, an uneasy chill settling across her shoulders.

Checking the survival kit she would need, she showered and shampooed her hair. When she would be able to bathe again she had no idea.

This was going to be different, she thought, echoing Brand's words. The criminals were going to give this their best shot; everyone was getting into the act. Not only the federal agencies but all the illegal dealers had gotten together, and this was a concentrated effort, spread out so that if one unit was caught, another or two or three of them would get through.

Taking the compact package with her, she locked the trailer and walked slowly to the office to wait for Brand. Glancing absently at the sky, she realized all the gray clouds had passed and the stars were massed overhead like cold sparkling sequins.

As she reached to open the door of the office, a truck turned into the drive—not Brand's. Surprised, she saw Ward Sutherland and Milt Spivey get out and walk toward her. She hadn't seen them since the setup they helped Brand pull on her not long after her arrival in Nogales. They were supposed to be on the surveillance, but she hadn't thought about their coming to Nogales for briefing.

"Customs Patrol's contribution to the Miss America segment of this illustrious organization," Ward said, bending to kiss her cheek as she stood with the door open.

"Hello, Beth," Milt said. Even in the semidarkness, his freckles were visible.

She smiled, following them inside the office, leaning against the desk as they greeted Alfredo.

"Brand should be back momentarily," Alfredo said. "They wanted to see him at headquarters."

Before anything else could be said, they heard the truck pull in and then Brand's hurried footsteps. She watched him as he spoke easily to the two officers and turned to look at her an instant before he issued last-minute instructions.

"This is what we *think* is going to happen. Be alert for anything. Varro is known to be heading the spearhead group that is set to enter the United States either in the Lower Rio Grande Valley between Eagle Pass and Presidio, Texas, or between Naco and Yuma, Arizona."

He looked up, his eyes meeting Beth's, but his expression didn't change. "We all know that Varro is as cold-blooded as they come; he has no reservations about what he does to accomplish his mission: murder, kidnapping, destruction—they're his weapons and he knows exactly how to use them to his best advantage."

"How do we know he's involved?" Milt asked.

"Beth and I were on a stakeout last month below my ranch where he was expected to cross the valley into the mountains near Madera Canyon again. We found one of his young troops injured and brought him in for questioning. He told our agents Varro's plans in exchange for asylum in this country."

Ward nodded. "A likely story. Easy way to get in here to infiltrate."

Brand smiled. "I imagine the agents thought about that, but with the information they got from him, they've been able to follow Varro. He's been very busy since he went back across the border to regroup."

He spread out a map he had and they all leaned over the desk to look. "Remember the 'Suicide Jockey' truck convoy in September? Well, they're sending another one through and Varro is suspected of being in with the terrorists who have plans to attempt to hijack that convoy. On our side of the mountains."

He straightened. "However"—he looked around at them and smiled with no humor in his eyes—"that won't be until later this month; perhaps in February."

"Why are we being briefed on it now, then?" Beth asked.

"Because we may still be in the field when the convoy is dispatched from Kirtland Air Force Base."

Ward drew in a sharp breath. "A month out there?"

Brand nodded. "We have no idea how many prongs the movement has nor how many different groups and types of materials are involved."

Milt ran a hand through the tuft of red hair sticking up on the back of his head. "My God!"

"If He's around, we may have to call on Him." Brand's comment was dry and an uneasy ripple went through them as they took in what they heard, scarcely believing. Stakeouts or surveillances seldom went on continuously for more than a week.

"We'll be reconnoitering near the Sasabe line and will keep in touch only as necessary with as little contact as we can get by on." Brand told them. "We rendezvous at the designated points every three days until further notice."

The two officers readied to leave and Brand followed them to the truck. She heard their quiet conversation and laughter without paying much attention. She was about to get a chance to prove women could make it in the Patrol under extremely adverse conditions.

Well, Smitty, here I go. Say one for me because female participation in the elite Customs Patrol organization may survive or fail according to my performance in the next few days, or weeks, or whatever it takes to track down this Varro. He's a maniac; he has to go.

She looked up as Brand came back into the office. He stopped to look at her a long moment and said, "Let's go, Beth."

Chapter Thirteen

Beth wanted badly to spit the sand from her mouth, but there was not enough saliva in her dry throat. She didn't dare move her hand to brush away the grains that ground into her pores. Watching the shadows cast by the mesquite that waved in the slight breeze, she imagined movement along with the whisper of the blowing sand. There was no one there; of that, she was certain.

Brand was fifty yards to her left in a small ravine that ran along the dry Santa Cruz riverbed. He told her, "I'll go along the bank until it curves. Don't move unless I give the signal."

Their signal was the soft but piercing cry of the tiny black nightbird that lived in the smoke trees along the river.

"Brand," she whispered, suddenly frightened as he started away from her.

His mouth dry and rough was hard on hers for an instant. "I love you, Beth." She reached for him but he was gone.

Shivering in the unusually warm January night, lis-

tening to sounds she couldn't identify, she was alone
in a hostile world for all the signs of life she could see.
If the smugglers or terrorists were on the move tonight as their latest information seemed to indicate,
they had picked the best or at least the darkest night to
move. Stars appeared for short times as thick clouds
shifted and the half moon was hidden somewhere near
the mountaintop behind them. An unusual dampness
clung to the desert wind.

She wondered if Ward and Milt had made their latest
rendezvous with special agents near Sasabe, hopefully
now on their way toward the bend in the Santa Cruz
riverbed as it entered the Coronado National Forest. If
the object of their stakeout made it to the edge of the
forest, they'd never find them.

The soft cry startled her and she stiffened. Brand
was not where he said he'd be but more in front of
her and must have gone farther along the riverbed
than he intended. She turned her head without rising
from her prone position, making a full sweep of the
rough terrain before she slid forward on her stomach.
The pistol in her right hand weighed a hundred
pounds, it seemed, and her own slight body twice that.
She was terrified, uncertain if it was of dying or of
killing someone else.

The men they hunted were killers and more, a fact
proven by the path of destruction the Customs Patrol
and other agencies had followed for months. They had
killed before and once more wouldn't matter to them.
Or twice.

Brand was out there. Ward and Milt. The agents. Jud
was dead, plus how many more she didn't want to

know. Her errant thoughts slid away as she listened for any sound. In the quiet, the weak call came again, still in front of her.

"Brand?" Her whisper carried on the night wind but there was no answer as she waited, holding her breath. She half-crouched on hands and knees to get around a clump of dried sagebrush, scratching her face as a stray prickly branch caught her. Her left hand, reaching ahead of her, found the drop-off into the riverbed. She held on to the edge, dragging her body around to get her legs over the side of the bank. Here, she remembered, it wasn't over six slanting feet to the bed and she could have some protection to half stand to look around.

The absolute quiet made her feel alone in an empty world. Where was Brand?

A soft mewing sound came from nearby just loud enough to be heard over her pounding heart. It wasn't Brand. Inching downward, her feet touched flat ground and, eyes straining in the near dark, she crouched there. Ahead of her, a shadow was etched against the blackness of the sky. What would be standing in a dry riverbed? Humped over was more like it. She waited, her breath rasping loud enough to be heard in Nogales, and the foul taste of deathly fright crowded her throat.

The thick soles of her desert boots made a soft brushing noise as she scooted toward the hump, gun held tight to the outside of her thigh as Brand had taught her, thumb on the safety to be lifted in a split second. She was a few feet away, eyes accustomed to the dimness, when she realized the shadowy outline was a car. The criminals could be inside. It was against her better judgment to storm the vehicle alone and she waited.

The soft cry came from the car and her body went stiff. It wasn't a bird call; it was human. Gun held with both hands in front of her, she inched forward. There was no movement or sound as she reached the car and she waited. In the total silence she wanted to scream for Brand, but that would endanger them both.

Kneeling by the back wheel, she shifted the gun to the right hand and dug into the sandy river bottom with her left, finding a few pebbles. She threw them and heard a tinny rattle as they hit the hood of the car. She froze, waiting. A feeble whimper came from near her left ear. Whoever was making the sound was in the trunk of the car. Holding her breath, she listened, eyes searching the dim banks on each side of her.

In a half-crouching position she swiveled, her left hand following the contours of the car wheel to the bumper and upward to the trunk. It was partly open. She felt for her penlight in the knife pocket along the leg of her fatigues, bringing it upward to slide it inside the opening before she pushed the button to turn it on.

For a moment all she saw was a small bundle of rags. The soft cry came from the rags and they moved a little. She turned off the tiny light, replacing it in her pocket. Turning her head to let her gaze take in the surrounding shadows, she stayed in the same position, placing her gun on the bumper of the car. She reached into the trunk, pulling the rags away, her hand finding soft baby skin, a thin amount of flesh over pitifully soft bones. Goose bumps covered her body and she was bathed in a cold sweat.

The piercing cry of the nightbird shattered the quiet and she froze, but just for an instant. She answered Brand's call, staring toward the opposite bank where she saw movement. The movement disappeared until she heard the scrape of Brand's boots and he was beside her.

"Beth?" He found her arm, squeezing tightly.

She whispered, "It's a baby."

His indrawn breath indicated the unexpectedness of her statement and he swore. They were looking for anything but a baby.

Brand's head jerked up a split second before she heard the snap of a dry piece of tumbleweed or sagebrush and he shoved her backward as he flung himself beside her. Instinctively, she grabbed the gun, rolling beneath the car at the same instant that a gun roared. Dirt sprayed them as the shot missed by inches.

"Get away from the gas tank," Brand ordered.

She started around the car toward the front opposite the side from the shots and remembered the ragged bundle in the trunk. She twisted, pushing the trunk lid all the way up. A second shot shattered the back window of the car.

"Move, Beth," Brand hissed, his voice farther from her now.

On her knees she reached to pull the bundle to her, dragging it across the bumper to the ground. She rolled it all together to keep from dropping the baby, pulled it to her chest, holding it with crossed arms, her gun held in both hands in front of it as she crawled around the car.

Head down, she looked toward the bank Brand had

left, spotting a clump of mesquite outlined against the sandy riverbed. She squirmed toward it, shoulders hunched, waiting for the shotgun blast that would send her and the baby into eternity. None came.

Breath hurting her chest, she pushed the quiet bundle behind the mesquite, turning without pause to wiggle her way back to the car and Brand. A pinpoint flash came from the bank and an instant later, the car went up in a whoosh, a fiery wave straight up into the black sky. She buried her face in the sand feeling heat through her clothing.

An unearthly silence was broken only by crackling flames. In shocked disbelief, she raised her head, trying to swallow over the terror in her throat. They would have killed the tiny baby without giving it a thought.

Terrorists or dealers in human flesh—she'd take the terrorists any time. Brand had tried to emphasize that this surveillance was the real thing. Real? No, it was unreal. Human beings did not do things like this to other human beings. Icy reality, tempered with anger such as she had never known, steadied her.

"Brand?" she called. Twisting, she went forward past the burning car; turning back to her right once she was in the middle of the riverbed. A loud rumble made her flinch as she waited for the burst of gunfire. It wasn't gunfire. Lightning split the dark clouds and the next clap of thunder shook the earth she was hugging tightly.

She was staring in startled amazement, and as she gazed two figures ran toward her along the bank. She raised the gun, hesitated, and lowered it. There was no sure way of knowing if Ward and Milt had arrived as planned. The timing wasn't exactly right, but she couldn't take that chance and watched helplessly as the two figures disappeared over the embankment.

Afraid of the tricks her eyes could play on her in the sometimes half-light, she blinked. To her right the blaze of the car roared in unison with the thunder and the first drops of rain cooled her face. Another streak of lightning split the darkness and the two men she had seen running were almost on top of her. One of them was Brand.

They tumbled to the ground, rolling, and she was close enough to see the knife in the man's hand and the evil grin as he poised to plunge it into Brand's chest. The weapon in her hand spit flames and the man's body toppled backward away from Brand.

The rain came in torrents now and she crouched trying to see what had happened, keeping her gun trained on the man who lay still a few feet away from her. The only noise was the rain and the sizzling sound it made in the diminishing flames of the car.

"Brand?" He was lying on his back, his face toward her in shocked surprise.

She heard a moan and turned away from Brand to see the man she had shot trying to get up. She raised the gun and pointed it but the figure slumped to the ground and lay still. After a moment she looked back at Brand who was sitting up now and she crawled over to him.

As she reached him, he made a sound and she looked up into his face, scratched and bleeding on one side, his eyes dark holes. He caught her close and held tightly for a moment.

"We have to get out of here, Beth. One of them got away and I'm sure there's more." He looked past her to the still figure and back at her, smiling a little.

It took several precious seconds for her voice to work. "Are—are you all right?" she finally managed.

"Thanks to you, honey." He was on his knees beside her, looking around through the pouring rain. "Let's get to that north bank and see if Ward's here, yet."

"The baby," she said.

"You don't have time, Beth."

"I can't leave it." She was away from his restraining arm, shoving her gun into the holster, half-crawling, half-running, her wet clothes grinding sand into her skin. Behind her, she heard Brand swear, but she was already by the mesquite bush where she had left the baby. She took the bundle into her arms.

His gun reholstered, Brand took the baby from her. "Run. There's going to be water in this bed in minutes."

Unhesitating now that he had the baby, Beth ran, realizing as she did that waters from heavy mountain rains could turn the dry riverbed into a cascade of murderous floodwaters no human could survive.

As they reached the top of the riverbank, he said, "There's a ridge a hundred yards back. Get behind it with the baby and stay there."

He handed her the infant as he started away. "No, Brand," she pleaded. "Don't leave me."

He didn't answer and she heard him slide down the bank and followed his shadow going toward the smoldering ruins of the car, swerving to reach the inert form of the man she had shot. Reaction was setting in and she wanted to scream, but she chewed on her lips and strained to see through the dimness.

A tiny gulping whimper brought her attention back to the baby and her arms tightened. She stared around her into the semidarkness, listening for any sound that would let her know someone else was nearby. There was nothing.

As suddenly as it came, the rain stopped, and she breathed a tiny prayer of thankfulness. Behind the low ridge Brand had directed her to, she placed the bundle on the ground and pushed aside the layer of dirty rags, wet now, her hands exploring.

The skin she touched was cold and clammy. The clothing was soaked and reeked of urine. Tiny fingers moved only a little as she rubbed them. She murmured softly as her hands went over its face and when her fingers touched the feverish lips, it sucked hungrily, making the soft mewing sound she had first heard.

Poor darling. How long had it been since the baby was fed?

Brand was struggling up the bank with his burden and reaching her, he dropped the man, his breath rasping in his throat.

"He's alive," he told her, dropping down beside her.

The coldest anger and hate she had ever known coursed through her, making her soft drawl hard. "Why didn't you leave him and let him wash away with his car?"

"He's a witness, Beth." He touched her arm. "I understand how you feel but we need him." His hand tightened. "We aren't out of this yet and we'll have to leave both of them here."

"No," she protested. "Not the baby."

"Yes," he said. "Both of them."

Her next words were lost in the roar of the water rushing out of the mountains into the dry riverbed. The rains had started hours ago in the higher elevations and it didn't take long for it to wash down the dry mountainsides, taking everything in its path. They turned as the frothing wall lifted the charred remains of the car and flung it into the air like a toy, where it hung an instant in the eerie light and was lost forever in the boiling mass.

Brand turned back to her. "Give me your light."

She handed the penlight to him from her knife pocket, watching as he shaded it in his fist to look at the baby's face where she had pulled the blanket back. Heads bent together, they looked at the pitiful sight.

"It's a girl," Brand whispered, fingers gentle as he touched the filth encrusted ears showing tiny gold dots of earrings. Black hair was matted close to the small head.

"Is she dead?" Beth didn't recognize her own voice; she only stared at the baby as she lay alarmingly still.

"No, but..." He let his voice drop as he covered the tiny face, dark blue circles under the closed eyes, lips blue and dry. He moved away from them and, using his knife, began digging a trench. The roar of the flooded riverbed suspended them in an unreal world as she watched him.

"You can't bury her," she said, her voice rising.

"I've got to. It's the only protection we can give her,

Beth." He stopped digging, hand poised with the knife inches above the shallow indentation he had made in the red sand. "Listen."

The shrill cry came a few yards away and Brand answered. Seconds later, a shadowy figure slid over the dunes.

"Brand?"

"Yeah."

"Ward. Milt's right behind me." A second figure moved noiselessly over the sand to be near him. "We heard shots, and what the hell was that explosion?"

Brand pointed at the man lying nearby. "Beth shot him. She's a darned good shot, but I think he'll live." He gave her a quick smile that disappeared as he added, "They exploded the gas tank in their car so we don't know if there was anything else in there we could use against them." He took the bundle from Beth and placed it in the small trench and pushed sand around it. "They don't deal in drugs or guns; they deal in babies, but we don't know how many. We only found one."

Ward's voice was tense. "Babies?" He swore quietly. Milt was silent as he digested the information.

"What time is it?" Brand asked.

"Three or thereabouts," Milt said. "Brand, two men got back across the riverbed, but we think there's at least one more, probably two."

"There was another one in the car and he could be one of those who got away from you." He moved to put his arm around Beth, trying to still the trembling in her slim body. "What are you basing the numbers on?"

"We were close enough to hear some of their conversations and it seemed to be three-way, but only two made it across the river before the rains came." Ward hesitated. "We were separated and afraid to shoot at them."

Brand nodded. "Let's go on with the plan. Tie him up so he'll never get loose." His voice was cold and hard as he indicated the silent figure a few feet away.

"He's bleeding pretty bad," Milt said, "Maybe we won't have to worry about him."

"I want him to live long enough to get information out of him," Brand said.

Beth listened, feeling nausea creeping up into her throat and she swallowed over the sour taste in her mouth. Brand patted her arm and hunched back on his heels, eyeing the clouds that broke away, leaving a shadowed half moon.

"We either interrupted the wrong gang or they've branched out into a more lucrative business." His voice grim, he went on. "Ward, you and Milt circle round the way we came, working up to point two of our plan. If we aren't there in thirty minutes, go without us and we'll regroup at point three. Wait for us there. I don't have to remind you these people are not shy about killing."

"Right." The two men looked around and moved away into the desert shadows.

As they faded into the darkness, Brand turned to Beth. "Are you okay?" His voice was hard without a sign of tenderness.

She shivered, wet and miserable. If ever she needed his tenderness, it was now, but he didn't have time for her as he fought for their survival. "Yes."

"Stay close to me," he ordered.

"I'm not leaving the baby."

"I don't want to any more than you, but we have to," he told her, biting the words as they came out.

"No. If I can't take her, I'm staying."

His move was swift as he caught her arms, yanking her close to him. "Let me remind you, Beth, that this is your job as well as mine and you're going to hold up your part of it."

His face, almost against hers, was tight, his eyes black in the shadows. She struggled silently. His mouth touched hers and their dry skin scraped as he grazed her chin. She closed her eyes, wanting him to hold her.

"I'm proud of you, Beth, you're doing fine," he said and his hands on her loosened. "Don't make it hard on both of us, honey. We've got to get going." He turned, pulling her with him.

A whimper from the blanket drew her attention, but Brand said, "No, Beth." He glanced at the still figure of the man Ward had bound and back at her.

"Please," she said.

He shook his head, half-dragging her behind him. As they circled the low dune heading upriver, he let her go, watching her a moment before he turned, crouching low as he led her away from the baby.

Her tears were salty as they ran silently into her mouth.

THE EERIE WHINE of the wind was the only sound as they went past point two. Ward and Milt weren't there. Brand's hand on Beth's shoulder held her down as he indicated with a wide motion of his hand that he intended to reconnoiter from where they lay. She hardly dared breathe as she waited till he came back and slid quietly down beside her.

He brushed her cheek with dry lips and whispered, "Let's go."

She followed him without thinking. *I'll always do what he wants me to without question,* she thought, and in spite of the circumstances she smiled. *Perhaps that's the way it should be.* She had not yet gotten around to doing as he wanted her to do by getting out of the Patrol. However...

Brand stopped a few feet in front of Beth and she waited. She too had heard something. Suddenly, a piercing cry sounded a hundred yards ahead of them. Brand waited five seconds and answered. They moved toward Ward and Milt.

They weren't alone. "Brand, you know Vance and Stokes. Brand's partner is Beth Page." Ward's teeth flashed in the half-light. "The agents got here just as we did, Brand, and we caught four men in a van that didn't make it past the flash flood areas. There are two more babies."

Beth's nails bit into her palms as Brand asked, "Alive?"

"Yes, but we'd better get them to a hospital fast."

"A helicopter will pick us up from the checkpoint within an hour," Stokes said. "Can we get the other baby by then?"

"Vance and I will go after it. We can mark where the other man is so he can be found after daylight," Milt said.

"How about the trucks?" Brand asked, looking at the special agents. The last phase of their surveillance had been a question mark from the beginning. Whether or not General Montague would choose to let the convoy of nuclear weapons and parts pass through their area now or hold them another month had not been decided when they received their last instructions.

"The shipment's been postponed, Brand," Vance told him. "The general wasn't taking any chances on Varro rounding up some of the FALN group to act as decoy while he took over."

"He's right," Brand said, his voice grim. "Varro is not in the ones we caught tonight and God knows where he'll show up."

For a long moment they were all quiet, thankful a part of the job was almost over, hot anger alive at the criminals for using kidnapped babies to sell to the highest bidder.

Beth moved closer to Brand and he slipped his arm around her. She leaned against him, exhausted.

THE SUN WAS HIGH when they returned to the office to find Alfredo with plenty of fresh coffee made. Brand filled him in on their activities since they had left him—was it only days ago?—while Beth slumped in a chair behind the desk, not listening as he related the part where she saved his life. Her thoughts were somewhere else even as she realized she was filthy and smelled like a wet dog.

"What about the little girl?" she asked.

Both men turned to look at her. Brand's dark gray eyes were bloodshot, dark circles under them. A glint of anger appeared and was gone but his mouth tightened.

"The babies have parents somewhere and it's up to

someone else to find them. We've done our job, but the babies go back home.''

"I thought..." She swallowed, passing her hand across her eyes.

His expression softened as he stood by the desk looking down at her bedraggled figure. He reached to push the tangled hair back from her face.

"I have a million reports to write. Go see if you can get yourself clean, get some sleep, and we'll talk tomorrow.'' He pulled her up into his arms, ignoring Alfredo's interested look.

"The babies will be fine and back home where they belong soon.'' He rubbed her back with the palm of his hand. "We have some planning to do for ourselves, don't we?''

She nodded, relaxing in his arms. He whispered against her ear, "You're a great partner. How about that lifetime contract?''

Tilting her head back, she met his dark gaze and she was no longer tired. "It's a deal.''

He let her go and she stumbled only a little as she left the office. The phone rang and she flinched, hoping it was only a query about the just-completed job and not another heartbreaking plan.

Brand's right. I'm not cut out for this, she thought, *but would I want to give it up?*

Her eyes searched the horizon and the dark forbidding rocks that stood relentlessly guarding the desolate country they surrounded. The cloudless sky framed the world in a shade of blue no artist had ever quite duplicated. A stiff breeze tumbled the dried mesquite, chasing it with red desert dust across the flatness.

It all housed the enemy, the unknown, the secrets of the land that had lain in wait for millions of years. In wait for what? For whom?

For me, perhaps, she thought, and walked into her trailer.

Chapter Fourteen

The surveillance and subsequent spearhead operations among the law enforcement agencies had netted a ring of the criminal element for which they searched, but Varro, the leader, had evaded all efforts and was still among the wanted. In the roundup of the ones they did catch, was the self-confessed killer of Brand's friend and neighbor, one of Varro's henchmen.

It hurt her to watch during the trial as Brand was forced to listen to the relating of the cold-blooded killing of the innocent young rancher. Afterward, they held each other tightly without talking and when he sought her love for protection, she was there and they shared the hurt and the healing.

Months had passed since the stakeout between Nogales and Sasabe had taken place and they continued their watchfulness; the boring, patient patrols that made up everyday life in the region they were assigned.

Brand's arms around her, his husky whispers, had pushed the shadows from her mind, quieted the screams that crowded into her throat from her nightmares. And as time passed so did the frightful dreams.

A lot of fuss had been made over the fact that she had shot one of the ringleaders in the illegal operations and in doing so saved Brand's life. She didn't let herself think about it, not what happened nor what could have happened had she frozen and not been able to shoot the hated pistol.

She would soon belong to him. As soon as the reports were filed from the last patrol, as soon as their leave papers were approved from headquarters and Ward was assigned to temporary duty while Brand was gone.

Married to Brand, she would still have doubts and worries but they would be shared. Not as dark and formidable as when you faced it alone. As long as they would leave her assigned with Brand, she could live with the uncertainty. With his own confidence he had already brought her more self-assurance about her place in the Patrol than she could ever have gotten alone. Maybe it wasn't where he preferred her to be, but she was there—with him.

Jim and Mary Ann had been quietly happy for them when she called to tell them and to say they wanted to be married at her home in a small ceremony. They didn't seem surprised.

Of course not. Beth smiled to herself. She had never been able to hide her feelings from those two.

Crossing the gravel drive to the office, she was smiling as she entered the front only to find it empty. Brand's truck was there, so he was around. She started into the back room that served as his office, stopping by the half-opened door when she heard voices. She raised her hand to knock, hesitating when she heard Ward laugh.

It was a nice easy sound—a sound she looked forward to hearing around the office because sometimes they were hard put to find anything to laugh about.

"Hey, Brand, I know you said you'd get her out of the Patrol some way, but I didn't think you'd go as far as marrying her."

Beth's hand hit the door and it opened back to slam against the wall, not loud but sounding like a shot in the sudden silence as the four people there looked up to see her.

Ward was propped back in one of the metal chairs against the wall; Milt and Alfredo stood by the file cabinets and Brand sat at the desk with papers scattered in front of him.

Brand hadn't answered Ward, but as their eyes met, she saw the truth without having to ask. The extended silence crashed like a roaring surf in her head as a one-second picture of the past months blinded her.

If he couldn't get her out any other way, he'd marry her? *How ridiculous,* she thought, simply uncomprehending. *Why bother?*

Making love to me was not the way to get rid of me, she wanted to tell him. *That only made me want to stay.* But it had been easier than their cold battle of wills; having a willing lover was just a side benefit from his campaign to get rid of her.

It was so plain that she stood, transfixed, staring at the group in the small room. It was so easy for him; she had made his task so easy for him, just by falling in love with him. His plan had been infallible; he had worked so diligently to make it a great success.

"My God," she said softly, backing through the doorway.

Brand was on his feet. "Beth, wait..."

"I remember now, Brand. I had forgotten, but you always did what you had to in order to get the job done. *Whatever* you had to do."

The shrill ring of the telephone vibrated through the room and Alfredo reached for it as Brand started around the desk. Her horrified gaze locked with Brand's, she turned automatically when the phone rang.

"It's Herb Crosley," Alfredo said and Brand stopped in mid-stride to look at him, his eyes blank for an instant.

With an impatient sound, he put his hand out to Beth. "Wait, I have to talk—"

Released from her frozen stance by his voice, she whirled toward the door. "Get her, Ward," she heard him order, but she didn't slow down.

She was on the last of the three cement steps outside when Ward reached her, grabbing her arm as she let go of the door.

Through clenched teeth, she said, "Let me go."

"Beth, I'm sorry. It was a j—"

She leaned forward, head down as he refused to release her, her shoulder catching him just above the belt. At the same time she yanked on the arm he held. He sailed over her, landing on his back in the red sand, grunting as his breath was cut short. She didn't look around at him but continued her long strides to her car, packed to the hilt for the trip to Brand's ranch where it would be left when they flew to Georgia to be married.

The midday sun was hot on her bare head, warming her back through her lightweight shirt as she walked blindly away from the office. Without looking to either right or left, she pulled from the driveway, following the narrow street to the intersection of Mariposa Road and Highway 19.

She made the familiar left turn going north, and just past the city limits she saw the overgrown rutted path their Patrol car had followed many times in the past months. The gray of her eyes darkened as she looked back at the shimmering asphalt of the highway.

"Turn right at Nogales, straight to hell," Brand had told her. She had to admit he was more than right. It would be a great epitaph on a gravestone.

A sound startled her and she realized she had cried out as the pain twisted through her and she doubled over the steering wheel as reality hit.

Lies. Every tender word of love, every kiss, every touch from Brand, all lies. All nothing but the framework of his scheme to get rid of the woman he never believed belonged in the Patrol.

Laughter bubbled up in her throat as she echoed Ward's statement: *I didn't know you'd go so far as to marry her to get her out of the Patrol.* She had to admit that was carrying things a bit far, even for a dedicated officer like Brand.

The car swerved and she straightened, turning the wheel to get back on the right side of the road. Thankfully, her mind went blank and she stared straight ahead at the empty highway. The sign for the turnoff to Patagonia loomed like a monstrous finger pointing in the direction she had planned to take but she didn't slow down nor give it more than a passing glance.

The intersection with I-10 came into sight and she slowed for the on-ramp, reading the sign that read: Benson—43 miles. The road she first recognized on their surveillance involving the truck convoy of nuclear weapons.

It was about that time, she recalled, when Brand stopped trying to persuade her to give up the Patrol. No, he hadn't stopped. He had just changed his tactics after a suitable length of time for her to become convinced that he accepted her whether he approved or not.

He had planned well for she had fallen: head over heels, hook, line, and sinker—and all the other ways she could have loved him, she had. Come to think of it, he had really started his campaign at the Academy and, with her gullible support, had made giant strides forward since that time.

He had accomplished all he set out to do—and more. Would he really have married her, thinking she'd give up the Patrol for him afterward? Well, wouldn't she have, if he had asked? Certainly.

Her short bark of laughter was loud in the car and she glanced into the rearview mirror at the empty highway behind her. In front was just as traffic free and she set the cruise control, easing her foot off the accelerator to stretch out her leg.

At Willcox, she pulled off at a truck stop; she didn't need gas but her throat was dry. Iced tea would keep her going for several more hours before she'd be hungry enough to eat. The way she felt now, she'd never be hungry again.

Taking a moment to become accustomed to the dimness of the café, Beth smiled as the young girl led her to a booth near the back. For early afternoon, the place was crowded.

Playing absently with the napkin and spoon in front of her, she listened to the hum of conversations around her, a mixture of Spanish and English. The sound was somehow soothing and kept her from thinking, at least for the time being.

She listened without meaning to, but it was only noise for a long while as she sat lost in her tortured thoughts of what she had heard Ward say. Brand had not contradicted him.

It took a moment for the meaning of the words she was overhearing now to sink in, and when it did, she stiffened. "Nuklier arma." Nuclear rebellion—or words to that effect. The conversation coming from the back booth was muffled, all in Spanish, and she caught only words.

"*Petroleo. Tomar.*"

A large glass of iced tea was placed in front of her and she murmured her thanks without looking up, trying not to lose the thread of the conversation in the booth behind her.

Her mouth was dry, her heart pounding as she interpreted what she had heard. A convoy of nuclear weapons was on its way from somewhere and would be passing on Interstate 10 in this area. When? She didn't catch that part.

Concentrating on the low-voiced discussion, she dared not look up to see who was doing the talking. As the voices continued, she made a mental picture of what they were saying, following with something like frozen horror the plan they laid out as if it were a Sunday drive.

The hijack surveillance had been called off. Varro somehow knew; but how? Their information network sometimes bordered on the unbelievable, especially when all the information they had was so carefully guarded.

Had Brand been notified that the convoy was coming through and would he be involved? Perhaps another team had been called in.

I don't want to go back to Nogales, she thought, *but if I have to...*

She finished her tea and paid the cashier on her way to the door, looking casually around the room to the back booth as she waited for her change. It was empty.

"Do you have a public telephone I could use?" she asked the cashier.

"Just outside, ma'am," the girl told her, pointing.

There were two booths, one with an "Out of Order" sign on the door. There was no one around as she asked the operator to put her through to the office, collect, giving her name as it was requested.

Alfredo answered. "Is Brand there?" Beth had been gone two hours; he could be anywhere. Maybe even celebrating the fact she was gone. Her soft lips tightened just as she heard his voice.

"Beth, where the hell—"

"Just listen. There isn't much time."

"Beth?"

"Is there a convoy of suicide jockeys due through this area tonight?"

He hesitated. "Beth, how did you know? We just got the message an hour ago."

"There's going to be a hijack attempt at the incline and curve about ten miles west of Willcox. I heard two men discussing the oil slick they had prepared to cause the trucks to skid off the highway. I think I understood them to say it would be near dark when the convoy is due to be in that area."

"Are you all right?" he asked quietly when she stopped talking.

"Yes," she said and went on as though he hadn't interrupted. "I didn't see the men who were talking and didn't understand if one of them was Varro or if he's the one in charge. His name was mentioned."

"Honey—"

"You don't have time to butter me up, Brand. If you want to try to catch Varro in the act, I suggest you move it."

She hung up the phone and leaned against the warm metal box for a moment before straightening and getting back into her car to pull back on to the interstate, heading east.

Just the sound of Brand's voice was enough to start her heart to pounding and she tried not to think that she would hear it very few times in the future. She had left her leave papers there and he could sign her out as of midnight.

I'll try not to bother you anymore, Brand, she thought. *You or Herb Crosley can arrange for my transfer out of your region. Surely Herb owes you that much for putting up with me all these months.*

Shaking away the icy realization that she was now alone again, when she thought she had Brand to have and to hold, she forced her attention back to the present. There would be plenty of time to be miserable about him when the long trip to Georgia was in the past.

She kept a lookout along the interstate for what she might identify as the convoy, but few vehicles of any kind went either way. It might be tomorrow night; she hadn't heard all the conversation and, anyway, General Montague could have heard rumors about a hijack and cancelled the trip as he had done many times before. She had done what she could to help; if it was wrong information, checking it out wouldn't hurt anyone. It was much better to check wrong information than to ignore it.

It was getting dark as she reached the outskirts of El Paso and she allowed herself the memory of the short time she and Brand spent there. The innocent looking brown building on her left that housed the El Paso Intelligence Center and Drug Enforcement Administration reminded her of her first encounter with the dark side of her job in the Patrol. There were not many light sides, now that she thought about it, although they had some laughs occasionally.

Brand was having the last laugh, she guessed.

A big billboard gave directions and distance to the Indian Cliffs Ranch and Cattleman's Steakhouse. Another milestone victory for Brand. She passed it all by and stopped in Van Horn for the night, sitting at the window a long time before she put her tired body to bed. Her mind was battle-weary, too, as she fought to keep from thinking about what she considered Brand's treachery.

If Brand caught Varro, that'd be a feather in his cap, she thought, and Herb Crosley would do whatever Brand wanted him to, including getting rid of Beth Page from his unit.

I'll save you the trouble, Brand. While I'm on leave, I'll apply for a transfer to anywhere they don't mind having a woman—if there is such a place.

Sleep finally came, disturbed by dreams, and when the baby's hands reached she sat up trying to get to her and woke, trembling and dripping sweat. It took a minute to realize where she was and that she couldn't call Brand. It would take a while to get accustomed to not turning to him for comfort when the job became a little too much for her. More and more, she realized there was another world people must struggle to live in.

She wiped her face on the sheet and turned on the light to see that it was four o'clock, lying there until her body stopped shaking.

There was little need to try to sleep any more and she found a pink cotton T-shirt and darker pink cotton pants, tying a wide pink-and-white band around her hair and was on the road again without bothering with coffee. She worried about what had happened to the convoy of nuclear weapons but knew better than to think anything would be on the newscasts or in the newspapers about it. Whatever had happened, the public would never be informed.

She could only hope and pray that nobody would be hurt. You got to the point where you prayed a lot in the

Patrol whether you really believed anyone listened or not.

She stopped to eat; stopped for gas; stopped to rest now and then, and finally she looked up to see a sign that said: Atlanta—38 miles.

The clouds that had followed her all morning lowered and the rains came, the hardest rain she had seen since she left Georgia. She read the familiar road signs to keep her mind busy but, still, it kept going back to the office scene from which she had escaped, unbelieving, but knowing there had been signs along the way to point to the truth she could no longer ignore.

Brand's dedication to the Patrol played a close second to his determination to get her out of it. She drew her shoulders together to ward off the hurt his determination had brought her.

"I'll survive," she said aloud. "He taught me to survive in the desert; surely, I can manage alone in civilization." She didn't need to go into the fact that she was filled with a world of uncertainty about that ability.

Finally losing her uncertainty about the job with Brand's help, she was back to questioning what she was really doing in the U.S. Customs Patrol, and weariness such as she had never known accompanied her heartache from Brand's double cross.

Jim and Mary Ann were not expecting her this soon, certainly not alone, and she dreaded explaining to them what had happened. They would support her and she could count on their understanding whether she understood or not.

The windshield wipers swished in a hypnotic rhythm. They seemed to say "No more, no more."

No more sleeping in the desert behind mesquite bushes. No more eating sand as the dust storms transported Arizona real estate mile upon deserted mile. No more Brand.

Glancing in the rearview mirror as she straightened, she looked in surprise at the shadows beneath her eyes, dark enough that she looked like someone had blacked them with a fist.

I didn't look this bad when I got out of the desert, but if I'd died there, it would have been in Brand's arms. Wherever I go from here, it will be alone—without Brand. Without sand dunes; without homeless, starving babies.

A breath shuddered through her, and thankfully she saw the road turning toward Dahlonega and the heavy traffic north of Atlanta thinned to almost nothing. The rain still came down in a steady pour and she turned her lights on for the last twenty miles of her journey.

Chapter Fifteen

She pulled up out of the water, holding onto the sides of the rough weathered planks, shaking her head to clear her eyes. It was too early for most people to be out swimming before Memorial Day and Beth had the lake to herself. She pulled up onto the boards and sat there, her knees drawn up under her chin.

As she had known they would, her parents listened to her story without interruption although she knew they exchanged glances whenever she hesitated or stumbled. Somehow, she got the facts related to them, trying to be fair to Brand without showing bitterness toward him.

It had taken several tries before she could give them the entire story, leaving out the results of their surveillances. Leaving out New Year's Eve. Telling them she wasn't planning to go back to Brand's outfit.

"You should have asked him outright if it were true, Beth," Jim said, "and let him deny what Ward said."

"I don't doubt the truth of it, Dad." She smiled a little, remembering the little tableau she had interrupted. "All you had to do was look at Brand and you just knew."

"He'll know you've come home, Beth, when you're not at the ranch, and he'll call," Mary Ann said.

Beth opened her mouth to say he would be occupied for a while, but she couldn't explain. She shook her head.

"I doubt it, Mother, but if he does..." She stopped. What was there to say that hadn't been said in those few enlightening moments as she stood before him in the trailer?

Glancing from Jim to Mary Ann, she said, making her voice strong and decisive, "If he calls, I don't want to talk to him." As Jim started to speak, she shook her head. "Why, Dad? Looking at it logically, why do I need to listen to his apologies? Brand's a gentleman; of course, he'll apologize, but he's off the hook so let him stay off."

She went to stand at the window to gaze at the unfamiliar sight of the rain still falling. "I want so much to say it doesn't matter, but it does." Her throat tightened and she couldn't go on.

They had talked on late into the night until she couldn't sit up any longer and she had slept, awakening with the bitter taste of tears in her mouth even though she didn't remember crying.

But in the days that followed, she did cry. Cried until the tears would no longer collect and fall, leaving an empty space where Brand's love had been.

The sun came down warm on her head and she stretched out face down, feeling her hair curl against her cheek as it dried. All the day before she had listened for the phone, but Brand had not called. She could believe that he was still on Varro's trail or that he simply did not want to talk to her.

Turning on her back, she stared up at the puffy clouds gathering to the west. Looked like the beginning of another north Georgia afternoon thunderstorm brewing over her head. She stood up and a moment later, went into the water with only a slight ripple left to show where she entered it.

As she dressed she glanced at her watch. Three thirty. She'd have plenty of time to get supper started before Mary Ann got home from the post office and Jim finished up whatever job he had going around the house or barn.

She had everything ready except bread when Mary Ann came in. "I left the biscuits for you, Mother," she grinned at her. "I can't make them the way you do."

As Mary Ann made the biscuits and popped them into the already heated oven, Beth set the table. Jim came in and, after a quick look at Beth, kissed Mary Ann's cheek.

Some of the color had come back into Beth's cheeks and the strain was gone from her expression. Her time spent at the lake, swimming or sitting in a dugout canoe, had added another shade of tan to her smooth complexion.

Jim patted her arm as she went past him and she gave him a quick smile. They were midway through the meal when the phone rang.

Automatically, Beth glanced at her watch. Four thirty, Nogales time.

"It's for you, Beth," Jim said, covering the mouth-piece. "It's person-to-person."

"Tell them I'm not here, Dad," she said and went on eating.

He hesitated then repeated what she said into the phone, coming back to the table, his eyes on his daughter across from him.

"It's not like you to handle things by running away, Beth," he said.

She raised her head to look at him. "I don't know how to handle it, Dad. I need a few more days before I can talk to Brand." She drew in her breath and put her fork down. "I've already written the letter to head-quarters asking for a transfer, preferably to Region Four, but anywhere besides Region Seven. If neces-sary, I'll go to Washington myself and see Herb Cros-ley. He's the one who—"

"I remember," Jim said quietly. "All right, Beth. I agree a transfer is probably the only answer right now, but..." Gray eyes, so like Beth's, were troubled.

DURING THE DAY while Jim and Mary Ann were out of the house, she stayed away too, going places she had gone as a teenager, visiting the places she and Jud had gone. The sadness for him was still there, but somehow the sharp edges had softened and she could miss him without the anger she had felt at first.

And everywhere she looked, there was Brand. She heard him laugh; she heard him call her name, felt his arms around her, his lips teasing, then roughly claiming her.

And Ward's voice loud and clear: *I didn't know you'd go as far as marrying her to get her out of the Patrol.*

The weekend passed and officially, she had been on leave one week of what was to have been a three-week leave. Since there would be no wedding, she could report back early if she got the assignment she asked for. If not, she'd stay the entire three weeks, refusing to think about having to report back to Brand.

She bought a book on quilts from the craft shop and left the small town of Helen behind her, heading home. Early summer was lovely at the end of the Blue Ridge Mountain chain. Warm, breezy days, cool nights. And the ever-present humidity. After the dry desert, she was having a time adjusting to the dampness always in the air.

It was Mary Ann's day off, and she and Jim had taken off for the lake to fish, promising to be home in time for supper.

The van wasn't in front of the house but another dark car she didn't recognize was pulled up by the front door.

Somebody looking for Jim inquiring about dairy products or a cow he had to sell, she guessed. They would be waiting inside in the living room, finding their way in through the front door that was always unlocked. Not like Arizona where everything was locked each time it was left unattended for a few minutes. In Dahlonega such precautions had never been necessary and it was considered unneighborly to lock a door.

She stood for a moment, leaning against the white pillar on the porch gazing across the tall pines and cedars lined along the front yard, and a picture of the barren desert framed by dinosaur-shaped rocks flashed in front of her.

Shaking her head at the hurt that could surge out of nowhere, she turned to walk through the screen door into the hallway, detouring to her right to see who waited for Jim.

"Hello, Beth," Brand said.

She stopped short in shocked surprise and couldn't speak as they stared at each other.

He looked tired. There was a slump to his normally straight shoulders and dark shadows under his eyes.

Her head went up before sympathetic feelings could surface. "Hello, Brand," she said and stood near the end of the couch close to the stairway. "Mother and Dad should be home shortly and—"

He shook his head. "They were here when I came and a friend called to invite them out to eat. Conveniently, I thought."

His mouth was a thin straight line, and though he leaned against the mantel seemingly relaxed, his body was tautly strung, ready for a quick move it seemed.

"I want to talk to you, Beth," he said. "And you either sit still for me to talk or I'll sit on you until I have my say. Jim and Mary Ann might not appreciate my sitting on you, but they'll agree that I should at least be heard."

"Have they already heard your version of the soap opera?" she asked.

"Soap opera?" His eyes darkened and he straightened away from the mantel. "Listen, Beth, you never gave me a chance to defend myself and—"

"You admit you needed to be defended? Even that's something." She made her voice agreeable with an effort, still not over his unexpected appearance.

His long arms hung at his sides, but she got the distinct idea that he was having trouble keeping them there. "You'd better sit down before I give in to the temptation to turn you over my knee and blister your behind."

"I believe there's something in the official code of conduct prohibiting that," she said, putting her arms across her chest.

He crossed the room quickly, catching her arm before she could move, pulling her down with him on the couch.

"Before we go any further, I love you. My thoughts lately have been anywhere but trying to get rid of you from my region. When I made the comment about getting rid of you, it was when Herb first told me I would be assigned a woman. I hadn't even met you at that time."

He was staring down into her eyes. He shook his head, mumbling, "I can't even look at you without forgetting what I was going to say."

"Did you get Varro?" she asked.

"What?" His eyes went over her face, settling on her mouth. He frowned. "You mean you'd rather hear about Varro than how I feel about you?" Suddenly, he grinned, shaking his head. "Maybe you're more of a Patrol officer than I thought, and I was already quite sure you were one of my best."

"One of the best?" She raised her eyebrows at him then leaned toward him. "Varro?"

He nodded. "When you called, we were just getting ready to leave. Informants had gotten to the agents in Douglas, telling them the hijacking was set for that evening but they didn't know where. Your information pinpointed it, making it possible for us to set them up." He waited a moment before going on.

"General Montague was nervous about the shipment and had a squad of special agents standing by so with the information you gave us, we had enough to move on."

He picked up her hands, closing his long fingers around them. "We got a dozen of Varro's men, as successful a haul as we've had in years in terms of its far-reaching consequences."

He straightened. "You can read the report, but I'll give you a brief recap. Varro escaped somehow, going down through the old Indian trail back of Tombstone, but agents were still surrounding Douglas and he ran right into their net."

"Did you get involved at all?"

"Yes. We met the convoy before it reached the oil spill. Milt and I were on the lead truck." He shook his head. "That truck driver is a cowboy. He made it look just like he was skidding all out of control and when the hijackers came out to get him, we were ready for them."

She let out her breath. "I'm glad," was all she could say.

"Aren't you going to ask where Ward was?"

At her puzzled look, he grinned, but the exhaustion was still in his eyes. "He had a sprained wrist and a very sore back."

"What happened?" she asked. Ward was one of the most agile of the officers she had met, and she envied the big man's ease of climbing and running as though he weighed nothing.

He laughed out loud. "Don't you remember?"

She shook her head. "Remember what?"

"He said he caught hold of your arm and you yanked him over your head. I thought he was stretching the truth a little. I know you'd remember doing something like that."

She gasped, recalling the blinding hurt and anger as she told Ward to let go, and when he didn't she caught him off balance, pulling him over her as she bent into his abdomen.

"I didn't know..." She stiffened and turned away. Whatever she did to Ward he deserved it. Really, it should have been Brand who got the sprained wrist; even a broken neck wouldn't be too severe for him.

"I love you, Beth. Am I forgiven for whatever you think I've done?"

"*Think*? Are you telling me that you didn't say you'd get rid of me some way?"

"No. But I thought you knew I'd changed my opinion where you're concerned. I don't want you to leave me, Beth."

"What about after we're married?"

He leaned toward her. "Then you do want to marry me?"

"Are you going to ask me to resign from the Patrol if we do get married?"

He was quiet, looking down at the hands he held, rubbing them before he faced her. "I talked to Herb before I left home. There's a regulation about husband and wife being stationed together in the Patrol. It's too dangerous." After a short silence, he went on. "I told him if we couldn't be stationed together, we'd both resign."

"What did he say?"

"He said I was threatening him." He smiled, reaching to touch her mouth. "I told him he was right." Still smiling, he went on. "He was quick to remind me that I was the one who didn't want a woman in the Patrol; that I fought him tooth and nail, and only consented to take you, screaming with anguish all the while. I admitted everything and after we finished hollering at each other, I asked for all our compensatory time we've stacked up over the past six months when we never had more than a few hours off at a time."

She laughed. "We don't have to go back to work till next Christmas, do we?"

He bent to kiss her. "That's just about long enough for us to begin our honeymoon, isn't it?"

She pulled away a little, but his arms tightened and he said, "Look, Beth, you gave me a rough time. If you don't kiss me right now, I might get violent just remembering what I went through after you walked out on me."

Her sharply indrawn breath was cut short as his mouth covered hers, his hands pulling her tightly into his arms, his fingers digging into her back.

Heart and body had not forgotten the effect Brand had on her, and she melted beneath his demanding kisses. As his mouth gentled on hers, he whispered, "How long will your parents be gone?"

She shook her head. "Not long enough."

"Oh, honey." He pulled her back into his arms. "I need you so much. You can't imagine..." He groaned.

"We could go to Dockery Lake," she suggested.

"Why?"

"We could go swimming."

"Swimming?" He pushed her away to look down into half-closed gray eyes. "You want to go swimming now? Beth..."

"Skinny dipping?"

"You know, darling, I feel like I've underestimated you all along," he said.

"I've tried to tell you that, Brand, but because I'm a woman you think I can't have feelings."

"I never said that, Beth."

"But you still think men have the edge on emotions as well as strength."

He kissed her lips lightly. "I'm stronger than you, Beth. I'm willing to allow you to show me how your emotions compare with mine." He stood up, pulling her with him, holding her body against him, making her aware of his meaning.

"How long will it take us to get to Dockery Lake?" he murmured against her mouth.

"Twenty minutes." Her breath was coming quickly as his lips caressed lightly across hers, his hands finding the curves of her body to fit them to him.

Everything faded as their kisses deepened as mutual investigation of their bodies brought renewed knowledge of the love they shared. Her eyes opened and stared straight into his as he slowly let her go.

Outside, a car door slammed.

"JIM SAYS WE CAN BE MARRIED Friday morning and have the van for a few days. We have to be in Washington next Thursday," Brand said at the breakfast table.

For hours after her parents came in the night before, they sat and talked. Brand told them as much as he could about the last escapade with Varro and his men.

"Why do you have to go to Washington? What's Herb trying to pull now?" Beth asked.

"The call I got the day you ran out on me," he said, giving her a hard look, "was from Herb. They had reviewed the full report of that surveillance where we broke the baby kidnapping ring and your part in it. You were put in for a couple of awards for saving the life of your supervisor as well as being an all-around outstanding Patrol officer."

She put down her fork, looking from Mary Ann to Jim and back to Brand. Her eyes narrowed and he saw the familiar dilation of the pupils as her temper slowly kindled.

"They give awards for shooting people, Brand? Jud dies for them; we rescue starving babies and round up hideous criminals and they give *me* an award? Just because I'm your token woman, Brand?" Her breath came rapidly, swelling her breasts beneath the thin blouse she wore. "What about you? And Ward? And Milt? And all the others that took part in all the shenanigans we pulled?" Her breath rasped in angry spurts.

Brand gave her parents a resigned look and took a deep breath before he reached across the table and picked up her hand, refusing to allow her to withdraw it from him. "Everyone will get recognition, Beth, but it was you who saved my life. Yes, it was your job to protect your partner and you did it just the way it was supposed to be done, putting the ringleader of the kidnappers out of commission for some time to come. Whatever you get from the Department, honey, you deserve.''

Brand turned to look at Jim, still holding on to her hand. "Beth insists on turning everything I say around to fit my opinions before she went to Nogales." He shook his head. "I never meant to fall in love with her. In fact, I meant to get rid of her as soon as I could no matter what kind of officer she was. Simply because I knew what kind of exposure she was sure to get out there. And I was right, Jim. It's rough.''

He turned to look back at Beth. "But I'm not going back without her. If they hold us to the regulation, then we go back to ranching full time. If not, we'll be back with the desert squirrels and any number of variations of Varro and his men if that's what Beth wants.''

Her eyes had come to rest on his face as he talked and the tender light in his eyes held her attention.

"One last surprise and then you can tell me you love me and recognize the fact that I love you and can't live without you. Smitty called after you left to congratulate us on our engagement—or to tell you she thought you were crazy—she hadn't decided which she was going to do. You should have heard her when I told her I had to go chasing all the way to Georgia after my bride-to-be. She knew that you'd be an outstanding officer and thought I deserved to be stood up.''

Grinning, he went on. "She and Ted will be in Washington for the awards.''

She continued to look across at him, not speaking, and he stood up and moved around the table to pull her up into his arms.

"Let's not waste any more of our leave, Beth. It's too short as it is and it won't be long till we're back with the tumbleweeds and jackrabbits."

She stood on tiptoe to kiss him, moving her mouth around to whisper in his ear. "We can go fishing at Dockery Lake this morning and be back in time to pick up the marriage license this afternoon."

He laughed softly against her mouth. "It's a date, darling," he whispered and winked at Jim and Mary Ann over her shoulder.